I0642596

Love Leave Live!

Domestic Violence & Gun Violence Can End!

Copyright © 2021 Melody Geddis McFadden

ISBN-978-1-7375549-8-1

Printed by Blessed Ministries in the United States of America.

First printing, July 2021

Dedication

This book is dedicated to the **MOTHERS** in my life. Bless God you!!!

Patricia Ann Geddis – My Birth Mother

Verona Martin Geddis – My Granny & My Forever Mother

Nevelyn Toot McFadden – My Mother in Love

Betty Cook Rhett – My Now Mother & Auntie

Pastor Marsha Buford – My Spiritual Mother

Bobbie Madea Boone – My Mother-in-law

Patricia Ann Cook – My Step-Mother

My Sister Mothers – Alice Denise Geddis Nesbitt, Songa Nikki Geddis McNeil, Vernia Sabrina Geddis Petty, Shawn Geddis McAfee

My Blessed Mothers – Patricia Phelps, Katherine Morris, Bevelyn Purham, Patricia Arlene Francis, Verdel Hilton, Renee Richardson & D'Orsay Harrison

My Auntie Mothers – AUNTS Delie, Tookie, Tina, Barbie, Jean, Deb, Marie, Helen, Mary, Mamie, Nita, Louise, Tina, Mattie, Christina, Clara, Johnny Mae, Lucille, Helen, Florence, Lizzy, Julia, Sis & every Auntie that loved me.

My Neighborhood Mothers: Pauline Thompson, Ethel Haynes, Daisy Brock, Eloise Vandyke, Elizabeth Tuug Lynah, Sadie Thompson & Mr. April Haynes

My Growing Up Mothers - Alfreda North & Jeanne Rutan

My Teaching Mothers – I. Manigault, E. Kinsey, M. J. Strickland, M. Davis, Reva Langford, Ms. LaBoo, Robert Smith, William Barnes, Tillene Erickson, Bill Young, Arlene Finney-el, Elizabeth Murray, Sylvia Gayle, Kate George & Mr. Carnegie CR Horton

Yes! I have needed a whole lot of Mothering from women and several men too! God has always supplied my every need. I could continue adding names but the list would fill this book. So my heart references each person that has loved me. I THANK God for each one of them because they have contributed greatly to the Woman that I was, the Woman that I am, the Woman that I will be and the Woman that I will be remembered as.

Sweet Smiles, Love Eternally & Every Blessing! ~ Melody Geddis McFadden

Love Leave Live!
Melody Geddis McFadden

Table of Contents

Dedication --2

Granny Tribute--3

Chapter 1: Curvy Cute Mama --------------------------------6

Chapter 2: Just So ---15

Chapter 3: My First--21

Chapter 4: Just Keep On Living! ----------------------------37

Chapter 5: Pray Careful--44

Chapter 6: A Hen Peck---50

Chapter 7: That Brown Paper Bag --------------------------59

Chapter 8: A Girl Is Born! ------------------------------------63

Chapter 9: An Old Soul---75

Chapter 10: Meet Your Seed! --------------------------------83

Chapter 11: Moving On! -------------------------------------97

Chapter 12: Churn Know!--------------------------------------102

Chapter 13: Real Enough? ----------------------------------109

Chapter 14: Old Sayings --------------------------------------116

Chapter 15: My Man? ---119

Chapter 16: Behind God's Back ----------------------------124

Chapter 17: Fake Fairytales ---------------------------------129

Chapter 18: Popping Gum & Spitting Lies------------------134

Chapter 19: Punching Bag -----------------------------------136

Chapter 20: Love Is Not This! -----------------------------142

Chapter 21: Forsake All Others! --------------------------152

Chapter 22: Oak Trees Don't Move! ----------------------163

Chapter 23: Rabid Dog In My House!-----------------------179

Chapter 24: The Eye Of My Storm! -----------------------186

Chapter 25: Crazy Gone? ------------------------------------208

Chapter 26: Jump Overboard --------------------------------218

Chapter 27: Crazy Is Back! ---------------------------------225

Chapter 28: The Bullet's Name ----------------------------231

Epilogue: Say Her Name!-------------------------------------243

Trr's Tribute --248

Author's Notes--249

Reflections ---256

Advocacy ---261-265

Chapter 1

Curvy Cute Mama

Black, a woman, southern, poor, curvy, pleasingly plump, ok man let's just tell all of that truth - fat. That's what people see... I always think about what they see. That's why my smooth, milk chocolate brown skin is always lotioned down. Vaseline on the lips, knees and elbows is the rule, Chile. Better believe, ain't no ash over here. My short natural curly fro is always combed, brushed and shining; can't forget to grease these curls. My makeup is subtle but always there. Accent the eyes, cheeks and lips and just maybe they'll be looking at my face instead of my fat. People always say how pretty my face is... like the rest of me sure ain't. If that's what they see, then fine. At least some of me is pretty. I might be fat to some but I always say that I am one curvy cute Mama.

So guess I work hard to keep as much of me cute as possible. I am always dressed real good. These hips might be big, but I make sure that they are covered, real cute like. If I don't find the right rags in the store, I know how to sew and I make my own styles. I might be the biggest girl in the room but you better believe, I look good; damn good. Those skinny girls always wondering how I keep the guys looking. I know the real secrets cause I listened when the old folks talked, "Catch dem Eyes and fill de stomachs, honey Chile". Yes ma'am! Works like a charm, every single time.

I make sure I'm never forgotten either. I cook the best food. Yep! That down home southern, spiced just right, finger licking, scratch made, good ole food. Plenty of the right seasonings just like Mama taught me and Girl, never forget the salt, pepper, sugar or the butter! They say I put my foot in those pots. Well if it don't taste right I'll put both feet and my hands too, deep deep down in there to make it just right. Ain't nobody ever leaving my table hungry and best believe they gonna be more than satisfied. Yep they will be wanting to come back every chance they get cause the getting is good.

My Mama taught me to work hard from the time I can remember my self. She explained, showed me and took her time with me until I got it. I learned better when I see a thing than from books. I get frustrated with all them big words on those pages that don't make no sense a'tall. I make Mama prouder than a hen that's laid her first egg cause I work real hard.

She always told me to do a good job. I kept it in the front of my head, that I must work smart and always work good. Well I paid attention to her cause my Mama didn't just talk for nothing. She talked when she had something to say. So when Mama talked, I listened, learned, obeyed and was the better for it. Every time I didn't listen I was the loser for it. Never failed if I didn't listen, it wouldn't be long and I'd wish I had. One thing sure, I learned that cleaning lesson. Learned it so good I could teach the class. Ain't many that can outwork this here girl. No sir. I be willing to work these fingers to the bone to get a job done and yep it's going to be done right good.

Ma worked cleaning houses for the white folks. She cleaned a house until it sparkled and shined. Guess that is where I got some of my "just right" attitude from. Man my Mama took such pride in what she did in them folks' houses. She told us that she did not work for people, she worked as unto the Lord. Yep, her boss was Jesus and his Daddy. So you better believe that she went above and beyond. Mama did the best she could every time, regardless of and no matter what.

I really looked up to my Mama, just like she was the sun, stars and the moon. I believed her and in her. You know without a doubt, that she believed, lived and loved that Jesus thing – no killing, stealing, lying etc. etc. etc... Yep she was All in. I believed cause Mama said believe, at first. Then some serious times came in my own life when Jesus made Himself totally real to me. So no I ain't beating down the Church door or nothing but Jesus and me got our own thing going on. I love Him. He loves me. That's that.

I really don't get off on all that religious foolishness. I just can't and I won't. Those preachers that only yell, scream and holler hellfire, brimstone, sin and death get on my nerves. Man, they work up a sweat and a lather just so they can pass the collection plate. They believe in telling people that the money is for Jesus. I always snicker when they say it cause I figure if God created everything and owns it all including them gold streets that people walking on in Glory, then what He need our pennies for?

Lord knows if they don't get enough begging, then like licking the sweet out of sugar, they try to charm the money out of folks. I tell you, it brings vomit to my throat when I think of those suave overly pretty preacher boys that see how many panties they can collect from those church ladies in their poor ole congregations. Boy when they do meet Jesus one day, it's going to be smoking! Man o Man! I smell hell's fire just thinking about it!

I refuse to sit up in those churches every Sunday and listen to their sermons about God is going to get you if you don't obey the rules and pay them all your money. Wraith! Fire! Hell! Brimstone! Thou shalt not! Thou wilt not! Thou! Thou! Thou! Well let me set it straight for y'all. The God that I serve is good, kind, forgiving and loving. He is a father. A good father that takes care of his children first, last and no matter what. He is a God that is all love. He ain't no sneaky liar, no money grabbing trickster and He is going to deal severely with all these play play so called believers that use His name in vain.

One time I was at Mama's house and me and some friends and family were heading to the club. I was taking my time and started getting dressed to go early. I was putting on my makeup, "just so", you know. And our girl who was 8 years old, was was standing in the doorway of the bedroom peeping. Those eyes were sparkling and the green was bright as emeralds, the way they were twinkling. I'd be rich if I could catch those jewels when they flashed by. She wasn't saying anything but I know when something is on her brain. So I finally asked what was twirling in her head. She looked down, shrugged and mumbled but said nothing that I could hear.

She still didn't leave which made me know for sure that something was bothering her bad. I asked again, she shrugged again but kept on peeping. Yep, this was something big, alright. After I pulled out my lipstick, I called her over. I touched it to her bottom lip and waited for her to rub her lips together. This was our thing and it always made both of us smile. I figured I would play along and calm her so I said, "Watch out superstar! Pretty pretty Girly! Don't hurt nobody with all that pretty!" She giggled and I smiled as I watched her in the mirror, still marveling that this little thing belonged to us.

She creeped a little more into the room as she watched me closely. I guess she finally got up her nerve. She bashfully looked in the mirror but never quite looked me in the eyes. She started speaking in a small voice that wobbled a little, which got my full attention cause this child was not scary. She wanted to know if I was saved. I started to play with her and ask, "Saved from what?" But I could see how serious this was for her. It touched me deep down for our girl to be concerned about my soul. So

I looked her in the eyes and told her that I know Jesus for myself.

I made it real clear to her that I ain't no Holy roller or nothing, but I do love God and He loves me. She rolled that over in that complicated brain of hers. I waited and watched it twirl. My sincerity and earnestness seemed to satisfy her cause she smiled that smile that lit up the whole room. I smiled with her and it lit up the lights in my heart. I truly understand now that when you make people feel happy you get some of that happiness right back and it's multiplied. That little thing stayed pretty happy so I was doing something right. Then she really touched me cause she said, "Don't forget that ever, alright?" I nodded yes as that happy washed all over me. She smiled some more and then bounced off with a book in hand to do her favorite thing; read.

I sat for a minute stunned that this little girl wanted me to verify my soul salvation. I decided to cement my talk with her by uttering a quick prayer asking God to receive me and my soul because I believe that He is real. I whispered that I believe that Jesus is His son, was born, died on Calvary and rose on the third day. It was important to say it with my voice to affirm my commitment. I could not finish until I ask that He forgive my sin and keep me as his own. I sat there smiling like some one gave the sweetest candy. I started humming 'how sweet it is to be loved by you'. Once that was settled a peace came over me that was like nothing I have ever felt.

This was one sweet, beautiful, smart child. But the wonder of it was that I birthed this little one. Every since she was born, I can't count the times, so many times, when I was out with her, people asked who's baby that was. When I said mine, they always gave me that look... the look that wondered if I was mental, stealing somebody's child or fronting and claiming a kid that definitely wasn't mine.

People followed me several times watching. They always acted like they were going the same way or that it was an accident that we kept meeting up. I got mad about it sometimes. Other times I just blew them off. If they were too pesky then it was their own fault when I told them real loud just where to go and how to get there. I was sure to offer help getting them there if they didn't get outta my face real fast.

I guess in a way, I should have been glad that they were being nosey. Children are taken every day. It's crazy people in this world and I know I would join the crazies if my baby was taken or hurt. Lord in heaven knows, if my child was missing I would want somebody to see where the suspicious person was going. I'm just glad I never caught a case because somebody reported a stolen child. Then I would have busted some heads killing the fools before they put me in jail for being out with my very own child.

I guest if I saw this coco brown lady with this high yeller, pretty near white child with eyes that changed from green to brown not to mention that head full of red, blond and brown straight hair; I might wonder too. Sometimes I added some water and hair grease to her hair. That hair would curl into the prettiest ringlets, you'd ever seen. I'd put it in a ponytail with a pretty ribbon and twirl those ringlets just so. The curls didn't make people think she was mine either. But she was. She was ours – me and my Mama's.

Chapter 2

"Just So"

Mama had a "I believe, I receive" attitude. I knew it was based on scripture and she lived it to the fullest. She was positive, optimistic and pumped people up even at their lowest moments. She raised me with that positive kick butt mindset. She always said ain't nothing I can't do if I put my mind to it and I believed it.

When I looked around in my life, I had plenty of proof that it was the real truth. Nothing stopped me once my mind was set. I'd find a way no matter what. As long as things were "Just So" everything would work out. Guess I had some Superman thinking, flying over tall buildings, knocking down brick walls, swimming the deepest seas... nothing stopped me once I got going.

Ain't had no money when my used cargo van needed some carpet. I got right down there and collected pieces of carpet from everybody and every place. Even checked dumpsters by businesses and trash by the road. Took a long while, but when I finally had enough, I installed that carpet, myself. Everybody said it looked real good too. Yep! They even wanted me to do their cars and trucks.

Offered me little bits of money or things they could trade. But man ain't nobody got time for that, God love them. I got me a life and I definitely ain't got no time to waste. Got my own stuff to deal with, every single day. I always laugh and say to every one of them, "I got to live out loud, til I die."

I like everything just so... Now y'all probably call it OCD, but I call it "Just So". My house at all times, yes that's 24 hours 7 days a week; looks like it is fully ready to be photographed for one of those shiny Home magazine covers that you see on the shelf at the grocery store and on the tables at the doctor's office.

I don't allow nothing to be out of place. I like to keep every single thing in order. Open a drawer in my house and all of the stuff is lined right up. Open a closet and every hanger is 1/8 inch away from the next one. Don't even need no ruler to measure either. I just know. I know when it's just so. The shirts are with the shirts, pants with the pants and all of the colors are right there together. If stuff is not right then I can't get no rest until it is just right.

People always saying that I go way too far with this stuff but I know what I like. I like it just right. They talk about me but when they get company, they always need to bring them by my place. Like it is a tourist stop for the whole neighborhood or something. They know that I will have cold fresh squeezed lemonade, sweet ice tea, homemade pound cake on the counter, a hot pot filled with good food on the stove, soft music playing to set just the right atmosphere and a welcome mat at the front door. Yep and it will all be just right too.

They laugh and talk cause I wipe my walls down regularly. I dust every single day. I hand wax my pretty shiny light Carmel brown hardwood floors. Yep, I said hand wax... On my hands and knees, little circles to the right to put the wax on and circles to the left to take the wax off. I wash my windows like clockwork, every two weeks; inside and out. No dirt, swirls or stains. No ma'am that definitely ain't happening in here. This is my place and I am keeping it just so. Nobody better try to change that either. I know how I like it and that is the way it is gonna be.

I know what and where every single thing is in my house. Ain't nothing can be hidden in here cause I am cleaning every crack and crevice. This is my place and if somebody wants privacy then don't bring it in here. My family teases me that I have spring cleaning twice a month. Probably do but it's how I like it and I ain't got no plans to change it.

I know I get crazy with it, but it's really what keeps me from getting crazy. If things are dirty, cluttered or out of place then I get nervous. Nervous ain't good in my world. I can't be accountable when that nervous takes over. I'm liable to forget myself and every single thing that my Mama taught me. I remember some days when ole nervous almost got the best of me. Thank God for Jesus! Lord knows that could have turned into World War III. But God! He kept me and saved everybody around me from me!

I was methodical when it comes to my house. I move my furniture two times a month to sweep and mop from under it. Can't let no dust bunnies hop in my fields. No not here. I rearrange every room regularly so that it looks like I got something new or different. A throw here. A new pillow there. Change the magazines on the tables even if a quick shuffle is all I have time for. Yep, I keep them wondering and admiring.

I have a green thumb so I had a ton of plants, veggies and beautiful flowers of every kind and color. Got a homemade hothouse to keep my plants warm in the cold times. Even in winter, I keep fresh cut flowers on my table just like white folks do in their fancy houses. When white folks dare to come in my house, they are always in wonder. I could look at their faces and tell that they were in extreme awe of what they see. My place is a marvel... Never fail here, cause it is always picture ready and picture perfect.

People was always whispering about how I do it. Well, I already know my secret. They always said I was a nervous child. When I would get in a mood, good, bad or ugly; then I would go to cleaning, cooking and taking care of everybody and everything. It keeps me calm when things are clean and in their places. Something aggravate me, I pick up a mop or broom. Somebody get on my nerves and I go to dusting. Not have enough food, then I get to planting, hunting, butchering or cooking. I just need to find a way and keep it neat. Clutter and dirt makes me real crazy. The last thing I need is more crazy. Yep, that is exactly why I keep it - just so.

I let my 3 daughters help so they can learn to work like me. Work good. Work steady. Work hard. 3 daughters live here with me at my house but I got 4 girls. Ain't no boys in me. No just girls. Got brothers that I helped raise. Guess that is as close to boys of my own as I am gonna get. Guess that's why the names or nicknames of my 3 girls are names that would work for girls or boys. That is probably cause I knew I was going to be a Woman maker.

Chapter 3

My First

My oldest girl stays with my Mama. She and my Mama attached just like me and my Mama – Attached. Mama said that this little girl will not work with her hands. This one will work with her mind. She ain't never lied and I know it is a good thing to believe my Mama. Cause the truth was in the mix for sure. I think that even the delivery of that little girl was so hard cause she came out with a book in her hands.

That sweet little baby girl was born different. Born under a good star with Angels on guard. They said that Angels were always around her to protect all that the Good Lord put in her. Guess we all prayed some of our hopes and dreams into her. We had such hard lives that we just wanted something to be good. That's a lot for a little person to carry. She was holding the hopes and dreams of a lot of folks that couldn't afford to even hope anymore. Lord knows dreams were expensive in these parts, so they were long done over here. But she was born to believe, hope and dream. Guess we all had paid the price with years unknown of pools filled with blood, barrels of sweat, and rivers of tears. The ancestors paid for this one to walk into the future with her heart wide open.

Mama and everybody that sets eyes on her, spoils that little girl rotten. Thank the Lord, she is good in her heart. She is not rotten, not bad, not a brat. Cause I would beat the bricks off of her if she was like that. Ain't nothing worst than a spoiled rotten, stinking, acting out brat! Makes me lose my good mind when I see them kids acting up, throwing a fit, falling all over the floor, yelling and screaming like they are off in the head. Lord help me when I see them telling their parents what to do in public. I'm real glad that she don't take advantage of people and those other good things the Lord put in her. I just hope and pray that she is as good as I think she is.

Family and friends sneaked coins into her hands that the other children didn't get. They bought little treats and smuggled them to her. The wonder was they didn't even get those treats for their own children. One of my favorite uncles always had something for our girl. Once he brought her a box, not one, but a whole box of candy. He had a whole passel of churn. Most people would say he had 3 or 4 passels. But he hid that candy until he could get it to her. He made a point to never see her without putting something in her. Even if it was kisses for her forehead, a kind word for her ears, a book to smarten her up, a piece of gum, a peppermint, or a leftover cookie from a lunchbox. No way was he ever going to not have something for her. Couldn't see her and not bless her with something. I prayed that it would teach her to be a blessing to others every chance she got.

It's extremely important, my Mama told me, that we always remind her who she is. She has been given a lot and a lot will be expected of her. I will do that. We all will do that. I'm glad that from the time she could walk, she is always trying to help people, so that's the good. Everybody don't have all the things the Lord trusted her with. So she better do right. She will do right long as I live that's for sure. It will be alright. She will be alright. I just know it. She is good dirt that I'm planting my hopes and dreams in. They will bring forth many good harvests.

I had her when I was far too young; only 17. One thing that I know for sure is that 17 is way too young to be somebody's Mama. Heck 17 is too young to date, too young to have sex, too young for much of anything. But here I was doing it anyway at 17.

I was sure that I knew everything. But I quickly realized that I didn't know anything about anything. I was young and dumb, looking for love in all the wrong places. He had a little cooler and after a few sneaked drinks out of that green Champale bottle (y'all know we couldn't afford champagne so we had the hood version- Champale). Once the bubbles hit my tongue, tickled my mouth til I felt like giggling. I could feel those bubbles popping and sizzling all the way down to my belly. Then add some smooth love music, a half white boy flirting that I had crushed on since the first time I seen him and we ended that night in the back seat of a car with my virtue gone. Unfortunately not long after, he was long gone too.

His old maid Aunts lived right across the street from us. His Mama's sisters that had helped raise him. He didn't even come back to their house after he heard what became of that 5 minute adventure in the backseat of his car. Those old folks sure knew more than we gave them credit for. They said over, over and over again, "What's done in the dark will come out in the light." My belly, big and round was plenty proof of that.

I had a time figuring out how to tell my God loving, Baptist from the floor up, Holy Ghost filled, Praying as her second, third and fourth languages, speaking in tongue as her fifth, knowing God, Jesus, the Holy Ghost, every single angel and the rest of the whole Heavenly crew on first name basis, Mama that I was expecting, knocked up, gone with the wind, pregnated. God help me, I was pregnant. Mercy God I was having a real baby.

Mama would be very disappointed cause she had warned me so very many times about what could happen in those back seats. I was the biggest fool ever. I fell into the old familiar trap. Quicksand was real and I had definitely stepped in it this time. I saw it happen to other girls but I did not think in a million years that it could happen to me. Well it did not take a million years, just 17... Fool, stupid, crazy me! I had a baby in my belly to prove that it could and it did happen to me.

My Mama was gentle, calm, kind, quiet and beautiful inside and out. What made her even more beautiful was that she did not have a clue as to how lovely she really was. She did not know that she was good through and through. She did not know that people wanted to be like her. Hell! A bunch of those mean, nosey old women that she carpooled to work with; wanted to be her.

She really did her best to live the Christian thing for real. It took a whole lot to get her to crazy. Trust and believe, that was crazy it was totally and completely, best not to see. I always said the devil himself had to show up to get her crazy. I had a hair trigger for crazy, but not Mama. She would get to praying instead of yelling. I just prayed not to kill anybody when the crazy was in full effect. I am sure that most of us got her share of crazy. She tried to pray it out of us but I think it was in there pretty deep. Way too deep even for the angels and saints to pray out. Jesus and His Daddy probably needed to lay all of their hands on me to get rid of all this crazy. It was crazy straight down deep to the core as them old gossiping hags used to say.

I really believe that Jesus and a team of angels surrounded her and kept her calm or something. When I told her that I was pregnant, I expecting some yelling, anger, even a slap or maybe a whipping but she just stayed calm and closed her eyes and her mouth. I know she was doing that "be slow to anger" thing....

She slowly shook her head and looked at her hands that were folded in her lap. Those weathered hands on this young beautiful Lady. Worn hands that cleaned houses, mopped floors and scrubbed toilets. Sweet hands that anointed our heads and combed our hair. Tired hands that planted, harvested, hunted and cooked our food. Exhausted hands that washed our clothes in a tub with no machine and hung them on a clothes line to dry. Old hands that stayed steepled in prayer.

She stared at those gentle hands for a long time. Then she lifted her head, straightened her back, pushed her shoulders up and looked me in the eyes. It felt like a hundred years passed in the few moments that she had stared at her hands. I could not make it if Mama threw me away. No, I would not live if Mama was done with me. I would not be able to go on. I would surely die if she turned her back on me.

I waited and realized that I was seeing stars and lights twinkling in front of my eyeballs like falling stars far away in a black midnight sky. I was holding my breath like I was scuba diving deep in the blackest ocean with no masks while the oxygen was quickly running out. Sinking. Sinking. Sinking... I was going to faint. I knew it. If she didn't look up soon, she would be looking down at me on the floor.

I was frantically looking around. I don't know what I was looking for. I could hardly see anything around me but I kept on looking. I just needed something to grab on to so that my whole world would not slip away. I just could not go on much longer. I finally focused on the wall above Mama's head. The white ceramic Jesus with that crown of thorns on his head had always made me feel closer to God. But right now I felt like those thorns were pricking my heart and I was bleeding out in the waiting. My bleeding heart was begging God to help me.

Things were getting darker and darker as I sank deeper and deeper into the incredibly pitiful, dumb, stupid mess that I had made. What was I going to do? How would I make it? Where would I go? Could I do this by myself? "Lord God, I just needed somebody, some thing... I don't even know what but I do know who... I just needed my Mama. Please Lord, help her to have mercy on me."

Couldn't blame nobody but me. No, nobody. This was all me. Could not even blame the dog that I had laid down with. I had been warned that if you lay down with dogs, you get up with fleas. Well, these were my fleas. Totally mine cause I knew better. I did. I really, truly, honestly, completely knew better. I just had not done better. But I would. "I promise you God. I promise. I promise with all of me."

"God, if you just opened my Mama's heart, I would do better. Please God. Please. Please. Please.", I kept praying. Every single second waiting on her to say something was a thousand years. "Lord Jesus, please don't let my Mama stop loving me. Father God, help her forgive me my sins." Geez I was so worried about Mama forgiving me that I realized that I had not even asked God to forgive me. Guess I was more scared of losing my Mama's love than God being mad about breaking His "Thou shalt not fornicate" rule.

I just wanted, I needed; I was desperate for my Mama to tell me that we would be all right. I know that I disappointed her with getting myself in this position. I know that I was breaking her heart for a few silly minutes of acting grown. I didn't think this through or I would not be here right now. On everything that I love, I knew that those few minutes in the back seat of a car would change us forever.

Mama kept her head down. She was a humble, but extremely strong and excruciatingly proud woman. When

I saw some tears roll down her cheeks, I knew for sure that I was totally dying. My heart was breaking in a million pieces because I was breaking her heart.

Mama finally threw her shoulders back and shook her head a few times. Every shake felt like a slap cause I was causing her this struggle and plenty of pain. I was causing her this heartache. That is the absolute last thing that I ever wanted to do. She flexed her shoulders like another thousand pounds had been put on them when they were already carrying the weight of the world. At least the weight of our whole world...

She carried the weight of so many and here I was pushing her back down into the dirt. I knew that I had added that thousand pounds on that Lady. Yeah, that was all my stuff. I did this and I regretted it from the top of my head to the soles of my feet. I know that she was strong as steel but I wasn't sure if she could take much more. I had seen her bend many times over the years but she never broke. I didn't want to be the straw that broke her back. Lordy! How could I have been so careless?

She lifted her beautiful hazel eyes that were filled with tears and looked my way. Every tear made me promise a thousand things that I would do to make up for this pain that I had brought to her. I never meant to cause her pain. So then and there, I promised in my heart to spend the rest of my life doing whatever I could to help her bear every burden, to help her shoulder every load, to block every attack, to fight every battle and to love her without measure. No matter what.

I was sure that I was drowning in the tears flowing from her eyes. I couldn't breathe. I was trying so hard to take enough air in. I just needed not to faint. The last thing I needed was to bust my head open.

I watched sorrowfully as she pulled out that little old worn cotton hankie with a bit of worn lace on the edges; that she kept in her bosom or up her sleeve. She loved that little hankie and it was excruciating as she dapped at those precious tears, sniffed as she daintily blew her red nose and twisted the hanky around in her work worn, tired but gentle hands.

I sunk deeper and deeper into the black abyss of sorrow as she stayed quiet for a while longer. I was losing all hope as each second went by. Father God help me! I couldn't even see the light of day anymore. All hope was draining out of ever hole in me. It was oozing from every pore as cold clammy sweat ran down every part of my body.

I know that she was probably praying. That woman prayed morning, noon and night. And without a doubt she would keep on praying until she got an answer or some resolve. She believed and lived out loud, that scripture: 'Pray without ceasing.' Heck! I know for sure that this is the 'ONE' day, that I was positive that she was not out praying me. If she could have heard all of the praying that I was doing, she would have been surely proud of me.

I was praying like I never prayed before or since. "God, if..." Can't say if. "God you are real. You are my Mama's God but you are mine too. So Daddy God, hear me. Answer me. Grant me the desires of my heart, Lord. Don't let her stop loving me. I can get through anything but that."

Boy she sure made me sweat that day. The sweat was running down my face in great waves. It was pooling between my breasts. It was moving like those white rapids that I saw on tv. There was no ebb or flow of the waters, just constant swells. Lord hurry up, cause all this water might cause a tsunami if we didn't do something fast, quick and in a hurry.

The sweat was going so fast and heavy down my back that I was sure when I stood up people would think that I peed myself. The chair that I was sitting in was safe though. It was fashionable these days to throw a piece of plastic over the chair cover and tuck it in tight. I absolutely hated the plastic chair covers but it was the style. So everybody was doing it.

Man, all this sweat would probably pour on the floor off of this plastic cover when this was over. If I lived, I would have something to calm my nerves cause the floor would surely need mopping. Lord knows I was praying that these dark muddy rivers of sweat turn into healing waters. I needed some healing waters. And I needed them right now.

Being the woman that my Mama was, she could never ever let me down. She was truly good. Every day of my life I was grateful for her. She straightened up and put that used hanky up her sleeve. She stood up and looked me dead in the eyes. She told me things that day that just made me love her all the more.

She said, "Sweet girl, every single day people do things that they are not proud of. All people made mistakes, they do. But not God. Never, never God. God knows the plans He has for you. The plans He has for this baby. The plans He has for us all. God will take your mess and make it just right. God makes every good and perfect thing. This baby will be a blessing. So hold your head up and put that shame and guilt aside. Nobody on this earth is sin free. No not one. We all fall short of the Glory of God. We just can't stay where we fall. Got to get up and get going."

It seemed like she was rambling on but I was grateful for every word. I had thought that she might not have much to say to me no more. She started pacing back and forth but talking in a calm voice. Almost seemed like she was talking to herself. She picked up the broom, started sweeping a little and that caused me to smile inside. That's where some of my just so energy came from when I was nervous or upset. Hadn't noticed that until today.

The broom sweeping was like background music for the words that she kept muttering. A lot of them went right over my head. I could not hear everything with the tsunami waters raging in my ears or in my head. Definitely didn't know which. She looked at me like she had asked me a question. I sat up straighter and tried to pay even more attention. She paused like she was in deep thought or listening to something that I sure couldn't hear.

The tsunami waves were coming closer. The black murky waters filled with my sins were going to crash over me any second. Mercy God! I can't swim. I was going to die. But then she started sweeping and grinning. I could not believe this. Wonder if I caused my Mama to finally lose her mind? Lord help us all.

She stopped sweeping and leaned on the broom for a second or two. Then she started talking again. "Girly, we can and we will do this together. The Lord is with us. He is on our side. Ain't no doubt about that. He will make a way out of no way. He would never put more on us than we could bear. It is alright. We are alright. Girl, I Love You! Now let's have us a baby." She opened her arms and stood there with them wide.

I got up so fast that I knocked my chair clean into the next room. I almost knocked her over rushing at her like a linebacker making the winning tackle. I knew it was alright when her arms closed around me. That was that. Signed, sealed and delivered. Didn't matter what nobody else said. No siree! My Mama had the first and the last word.

She had said that she would be there to help. So she would. With her on my side, I knew we would be alright. I was not in this alone. Mama was my own personal angel. She would get me through this. All of the stress and turmoil inside of me, faded away like fog as the heat of the day rolled in. I took a long, deep, soothing breath. As they sung in church, I was now singing in my heart, "I've got a feeling, everything gonna be alright."

Chapter 4

<u>Just Keep On Living!</u>

I was used to raising churn, we still had a house full of my brothers and sisters, so that was never the thing that bothered me. Babies were fine. I knew exactly how to take care of babies. Had been doing it all my life. My baby sister was only two and I had just finished potty training her.

So I knew all about babies. That the halfbreed shit that I had sex with only one time, left me holding the bag and the baby. All that was true. Very true but it was no big deal. With my Mama on my side, I figured that I got this. I got some peace. I even got some happy. Thanks be to God and to Mama.

At least a little bit of happy is better than none. Considering that I still was going to get those knowing looks and sly whispers when I walked by those old nosy neighborhood gossips. That's okay, cause it ain't like many of them ain't been in this same trouble. They knew exactly what size these shoes are. A bunch of them had their own personal pairs hidden in their closets or under the bed. They know exactly what these shoes feel like cause they had worn them a time or two or three themselves.

So they could act uppity and better than, if they want to. I would be sure to knock them right off of their high and mighty thrones if they got up in my face or caught me at a bad time. Those thrones were rickety and broke down anyway; to everybody looking in. The only people confused about what it was; is those old bitties that were used to acting uppity as they sat, judging and holding on for dear mercy. No body wanted their rusty old thrones.

Trust and believe I been wanting to knock some of those old hags' heads off anyway. Their perches had held them up for a very long time. If they mess with me that crazy just might visit. None of them wanted that. That is for sure. If they were not careful, I just finally might get my chance! No worries, they already know just who and who not to play with – me!

Once my Mama knew that we were pregnant, I started wondering what our baby would look like. Here is what I do know, it's our baby; me and my Mama's baby cause it is definitely a thousand percent not his. His who? The sperm giver, donator runner and the lowdown coward, that's who. Yeah this baby has his dna but it is definitely not his. He didn't want no part of it. So he wasn't getting none either. And I mean that with everything in me.

The minute that he denied my baby, that was it. Totally, completely, thoroughly done. I was through with him forever and ever, amen. They used to say that there is a thin line between love and hate. Apparently I had raced through that line like a runaway freight train coming down a wet mountain track. Cause I was definitely on the hate side of the track.

Mama had always said, "Just keep on living, you will understand it better by and by." Guess I should say that the by and by came. Cause today I can honestly say that I understand. She told me that if I just listen, then the lessons won't be difficult. Yep! A hard head makes a soft behind. And I got one big soft behind.

Now I know me. See, I loved hard but I hated hard too. The same way I loved with every fiber of my being, I hated the exact same way. Maybe even more if I had to be honest about it. I had a special place in my hate space for anybody that did children wrong. I hope there's a extra hot place in the bowels of hell for people that neglected or abused children.

The donor was doing me wrong and that was bad. But worst than anything else in the whole wide world was him denying and neglecting this innocent little baby. Could even get technical enough to consider it emotional and physical abuse. He was never going to meet her Daddy needs. And I know he was not going to bring money for her physical needs either.

Can't even imagine the hours that this child would spend thinking of reasons that the Bastard didn't want to be it's Daddy. Who would do that except a selfish old dog like that one I laid down with. He could keep making excuses to his family members about it not being his. He could lie to his friends that he had not had sex with me. He didn't have to own my baby before the world. But God knew the truth and he did too.

I hoped that some day he would realize just how lowdown he was. I hoped he figured it out before this baby started asking who, what, when, why and where. Cause he best believe that I would never lie for him. I was going to tell the truth about what he did or didn't do.

If he wanted a different story told then he had better put some different cards on the table. All I knew is that he was sure that I had a losing hand. But just like a professional poker player I was bluffing good. In the end I would win cause I stayed in this child's life. He would be so very sorry, some sweet day.

I know that he would be thirsty one day and this is the very child that he would have to ask for a drink of water. The child might turn its back. It might toss dirty water his way. Hell it might spit on his sorry butt. All I know is that if he was on fire, I would not spit on him to put it out. I'd be yelling, "Burn boy burn!"

I know Mama and God did not want me to be like that but God knows my heart and that is exactly what is in it. I told his spinster Aunties that were my neighbors the same things too cause that scaredy cat never did come around during the pregnancy. Didn't want to put them in my business but I wanted to be sure that the message got to him. If he fell off the side of the earth that was plenty fine with me. Just seeing the coward, probably would have made me violently throw up anyway or at least make me want to beat the tar out of him. But no! I couldn't let this one tempt me cause I didn't want this child born in jail. Mama would never forgive me for that so I better hold my piece.

When I loved, I loved. When I hated, I did that too. No since in doing things halfway. It's all or nothing in my book. Ain't no middle ground in this field. I'd rather plow the whole ground when I got started. That damn "denying my baby" messed up fool could go straight to hell with gasoline drawers on. I'd borrow money from the loan sharks or pick up cans and bottles to sell for extra gas to pour on the fire. Wouldn't want the fire to go out with him in it. No! I ain't playing at all. Not when it comes to me or mine. He didn't have to come near me or my baby ever. And I mean that with everything in me. My baby would be just fine without him. Bet that!

I am serious about this stuff but I am not unreasonable; at least not in my opinion. If some day, my baby wants to see the donor, then I will try hard not to stand in the way. I won't, really. I know me, so yes; I will be pissed. Pissed as all get out, I'm sure. Extremely pissed. Hellfire pissed. Ain't no doubt about that. Can't lie. Cause anybody that knows me will be hauling tail, if and when that day comes. I will be ready and waiting to pull his testicles out through his nose with no anesthesia.

Men weren't what they used to be. No not these days. It was sad and shameful. It left girls like me to realize that it was the way it was. It left me holding the whole bag. A bag that I hadn't bargained for. These guys were all about themselves. Not to mention forgetting the responsibility that they were supposed to help shoulder. Can't blame their parents and families, it was all on them. Selfish, self serving choices that left other people to deal with their stuff. Total boys in grown men's bodies.

So many men did it so selfishly these days. They wanted to have the fun but didn't want to rock the cradle. He hadn't wanted me or the baby. But good thing for him and for me; my Mama was in the picture. He had no clue that my Mama was saving his worthless life. I wasn't killing him cause she was in my corner. I know how to do what is best for others, after all look who my Mama is. She taught me good; real good. So I will do good. I'm going to make sure that I stay far away from him so that I am not tempted. Won't give the devil no room. Learned that lesson already and I am not going back to that class again. So now that I know better; I do better.

Chapter 5
Pray Careful

Mama was breathtakingly beautiful. She acted like she didn't even know it. Her mother was Black, negro, colored; however you want to put it. It all works. Her father was a Native American Indian of the Cherokee Nation. Mama had light creamy skin and shiny soft black hair that reached all the way down her back. She never flaunted that gorgeous hair. I know if I had it, I would never have put that hair up. Her every day hairdo was a swept bang on the side with most of it in a bun at the nape of her neck. The only time she let that beautiful hair down was for church on Sunday, a wedding or a funeral.

I loved it when she called one of us girls and handed us her old wooden brush. She sit in the chair, lay her head back with that beautiful hair flowing. We would fight to brush her hair in the evenings. It was soft and black as night. If it wasn't my turn to brush, I would still watch. I know that it was relaxing for her but it relaxed us too. When we were done brushing her glorious hair, we braid it in one or two braids for her to sleep.

When I figured out that I was going to have a baby, one of my first prayers was that my baby would have hair like that. It didn't need to be that long or that black just be soft and straight like Mama's. I guess I should have considered if it was a girl or boy but it didn't matter to me. I just wanted my child to look, act and be like Mama.

I prayed hard that my little baby, girl or boy, would look like my Mama. I thought it. I talked about it. I dreamed it. I was doing everything that I could to manifest it. Mama always told me that as you think, you are. So I kept thinking.

It's sad to even think about it but we live in a warped world. Twisted and off in a lot of ways. Things that should not matter, do. Skin color and hair texture should be embraced for its unique beauty. Instead it always seemed that we were being judged. Judged for many things that we have absolutely no control of. Some things that we would change in a flash if we could. Except that we could not.

Probably make things a little easier on the baby in this tilted world that we live in. Prejudice is real. And it's not just a black and white thing. It is real in the black community too. Sometimes it is more seen and felt from our own folks. We called each other names that we would be ready to fight over if someone from another race even thought less more said out loud. We said inexcusable things about skin color, noses, lips, legs, butts and hair.

Those slave masters had taught our people well cause we were still using their tactics to divide us, to deny us and to keep us down. Like crabs in a barrel, we spent way too much time pulling each other down in the muck. We should have been admiring our specialness instead we constantly put ourselves down. We compared each other and judged ourselves harsher than the hardest judges.

We don't stand up for ourselves and definitely not for others in our communities. This poison seemed to radiate like venom from the fangs of a rattle snake that bit us a very very long time ago. No healing serum worked to rid us of this life threatening infection. This sickness oozed like puss from a wound that had not been cared for at all. Now we have been infected for so long, it was a way of our lives. No cure could be imagined or thought of because nobody was looking for one. We got used to living with the sickness.

It was our way so nobody batted an eye when people called one another by a vile name and hid it in the throes of affection. Sad and unpleasant cruel names became nicknames. A lot of the times we forgot the real name in lieu of those awful nicknames. Nappy, Blackie, Niggy, Darkie, Fat Fat, Biggie and Nosey all lived in our neighborhood.

Just like back in slavery times, that brown paper bag was still evident in every community; especially and sadly in the black neighborhoods. Some people used it as a ruler. Others used it as a binder and many used it as punishment. If you were lighter than the bag, it was better for you. If you were darker than the bag then it was harder. I know that I was ready to burn that bag on too many occasions to count.

People lighter than the bag was able to join clubs and get certain positions. They even held desired jobs for people that beat that bag. It was sad that people tried hard to do whatever they could to beat the bag. Bleaching creams, potions and lotions were treasured. Many folks didn't dare go outside until the sun went down for fear of turning darker. If they did long sleeves and umbrellas in blazing heat was not unusual.

This life was a fight. Every day there were battles. Things said and unsaid. Seen and unseen. But the fight was real. I figured that this baby would probably do better if it was light skinned. The lighter, the better. I know it was not exactly right but I have seen the difference, my whole life. I'm not light. That bag had slapped me on too many occasions to count.

So I wanted my baby to have every advantage. Even though it might be hard on some levels, it would be best to not have to fight every battle. Not fighting white folks was probably the easiest fight. Even though fighting black folks was always going to be on the table, it just seemed easier to fight the devil you know. I didn't want my baby to have to fight any devils to tell the truth.

I know that I don't have any real say so. You get what you get. That's the fact of things. We take what God gives us. And I do know that He gives us just what we need. In my heart I pray and hope that my child agrees. I been fighting that paper bag for a very long time so I didn't want my baby to engage in this senseless battle. Even though black folks will most likely give her some grief, she would make out better in this white world. At least that's how I see it.

I could hear the names now that they called light skinned black people, "Cracker, Whitey, Red bone, Banana, Light skinned, Light bright – damn near white". Names and all, I still think it was still best this way. All my life, I'd been called names. "Fatty, chubby, Blackie, pickaninny, gal, girl, picky head and so many other things."

How ever this worked out, I knew from here on out to pray careful; real careful. Cause those old sayings were biting me in the butt again. They always used to say, "Be careful what you pray for." I sure will. No doubt about that.

I will never forget the 'N' word. Names hurt. Words hurt. They always used to say that names and words won't break bones. But I am here to tell you that they do break hearts. Life hurts too. It hurts real bad. We need every bit of help we can get, every time we can get it; to make it in this sad world.

Chapter 6

A Hen Peck

My first child, my own baby, came into this world after a very long grueling day of labor. The house was filled with women. Women of all shapes, sizes and colors. They came from near and far when the call went out that somebody was in labor. I was in my parents big queen sized bed suffering. I was crying my head off. With everything in me, I was trying hard not to curse in front of the church ladies and shame my Mama. I was doing my best to live up to the grown woman that I fooled myself into thinking that I was. At least I had thought that when I got into the backseat of that car with the sperm donor.

All them ladies that knew me and Mama, figured a baby being born was the perfect time for a Hen Peck. That's what they called the ladies getting together around a birth, a death or some tragedy in the community. I'm sure that some man gave the gathering it's name. But those ladies and girls didn't care as long as the house was full, the food was good, there was plenty to drink, the singing was soulful, the company was lively and the gossip never stopped flowing.

Soon as word got out that someone was in active labor, they grabbed all of the women folk and their daughters. Here they'd come carrying cakes, cookies, casseroles, salads, fresh fruit, vegetables from their gardens, fresh squeezed lemonade, sun tea, iced coffee and anything else that they had. No one came empty handed. They took their littles, put them together and made lots. Long as the labor lasted, they kept the peck going which meant plenty of good cooking, eating, drinking and gossiping.

I'd been to many Pecks with Mama over the years. I always thought they were enjoyable. The food; all of that glorious food and so much fun and games. We'd eat, play games, eat, fix hair, eat, gossip and eat some more. Yeah I looked forward to a good Peck!

I had never thought much about the person who was screaming at the top of their voice during the Peck. I was too busy eating and having fun. It had always been so much fun; when I was not the one in the bed delivering the baby. It was a whole different thing from this point of view. That's for sure!

When the Ladies got too rowdy with the gossip or I got to laboring real loud, one of those church ladies would break out in a loud moving prayer or strike up a good old church song. Everybody would join in all through the house. It was like a wave of soothing calm that moved through on the notes that flowed from room to room. Lord knows before long the Holy Ghost would be up in there with all those Ladies singing from deep down in their souls.

Man oh man! They would start clapping, foot patting, tapping and stomping. Then the tears would start flowing. Some of the Ladies laughed, waved, rocked, walked, twirled in circles and even jumped or ran around if the spirit hit them.

Us girls had always peeked at them and then mocked the ones that we thought were the funniest. We'd do just like the Ladies and join hands in a circle so the girls could jump, dance and shout. The circles kept them from bumping into furniture or falling and hurting themselves.

We really went far in mocking those church Ladies. It was normal for one or two that would fall on the floor. The old preacher used to say that they was slain in the spirit. He said that God had to get them quiet so that He could speak to them. He said that God performed surgeries in the spirit and repaired hurt places or downloaded info that they would need for their journeys.

The other Ladies would throw a sheet across the one on the floor to protect her modesty. Then they would stand watch, praying and waiting. When a Lady fell, one of us girls would fall. We'd throw a towel or a jacket across her legs and we'd laugh and giggle until the girl got back up. I wish I was out there; instead of in here today. But nope! A few stupid minutes in a backseat meant that I'm in here screaming my lungs out and they are out there laughing and having a fricking party.

I had a favorite part of every single peck that I had ever attended. Without fail, it was always the humming. Those singing Ladies could lay it down when they got going. But no matter what, the song was not over til the Ladies put in a round or two of humming.

Lord knows that the humming was good. It was the craziest thing ever that they even hummed in tune. The sopranos hummed high. The altos held the middle with pride. Some Ladies had those deep voices so they handled the tenors part with gusto. The humming ran over my skin like cool water on a hot summer's day.

Since my guts was being ripped apart with every single contraction and I was surely dying an excruciating, slow, torturous death. The humming rocked me slow and easy. It was soothing to my soul when I needed it most. Cause if I had not known Jesus before that day, I definitely would have by the time my tiny baby made it into this world.

The old people were always telling us all about their life experiences. "Remember when..." "Was a time when..." "When I was young..." "In the old days" "Back when". We took all of what they said with a grain of salt. Meaning we acted like we was listening. But truth be told, we didn't listen to much that they said. It seemed like a waste of time, especially when they said the same thing over and over. What we didn't realize was that those words were being planted deep in us. At the weirdest times, those same words would pop up out of no where. And most times it was when we needed them most.

We were young, silly and full of ourselves not to mention that we were running over with attitude; especially when they started talking about the old days. Giggles, mocking, funny faces, neck popping and eye rolling when we could get away with it was common. Didn't want to get caught disrespecting your elders cause a "Come to Jesus" meeting would be happening right fast. Everybody knew that those meetings were based on the scriptures - spare the rod, spoil the child. Plenty of rods all about so ain't many spoiled children round here. Definitely couldn't find none in our house.

If they wanted to get rid of all the young ones, all they had to do was spit a bit of wisdom. Lord knows when they started with, "Back in the day..." everybody cleared out, fast, quick and in a hurry. Suddenly those chores needed doing right now. Homework couldn't wait a minute longer. Had to get somewhere right then. Didn't want to hear that same old stuff from the old folks again!

Now that I am laying here with nothing to do but holler, cry and birth this baby that seemed like it was taking forever and a day to come; I realized some evident truth. Y'all know that them old people sure do know what they are talking about. They know a whole lot. A whole lot that I didn't give them credit for.

I fully understand now my Mama's favorite saying, "Just keep on living, you'll understand better by and by." She said it so much that when she said "Just keep"; we all would chime in with the rest. She would smile and shake her head. We should have paid more attention to those smiles and especially to the head shaking.

Yep, them ole sayings, that sounded crazy and unbelievable; now I knew for myself that it was all truth. Man all those old says were rolling in this birthing room like a high tide. I was drowning in the words. One after another those old sayings were creeping in the room to peek and laugh at my behind. It's like they were licking their tongues out and mocking me and my know it all self. Now I knew why, every time we turned around, they always told us, "Better be careful what you pray for, cause you just might get it."

I'd prayed. I'd asked. I just didn't expect for God to come through for me, at least not that much. He was really listening that time. Probably laughing His head off too. God has a sense of humor and it shows up all the time in the answers to our prayers. Every time we are reminded of the prayer that got us to a certain place; I can just imagine that God, Jesus, the Saints and the angels in attendance are busting a gut; laughing. Probably tears running down their faces as they choke on their glee over our foolishness.

I prayed. Always had. Who couldn't with a Mama like mine. I just never knew that He heard me like that. When I realized that He wasn't just listening, He was listening to me; I was astounded. So I started laughing. Laughing my head off at me. Laughing like I had lost my true loving mind. I figured if He was laughing at me, I would laugh too. Laugh now cause just looking at the answers to my prayers made me know that I would be crying a whole lot later.

I have always known that my Mama's prayers were answered. She kept a book with prayer requests and dated it at the ask and the answer. She always said that it strengthened her faith to see how many times He heard and answered. She wrote little notes by the requests that others would have considered not answered. The notes usually included how things worked out for her good or the good of others concerning the requests. The notes sometimes included praise, amazement, questions, gratitude and wonder. But without fail, the notes included these words, "Thank You Daddy-God".

It was stunning and mind blowing but He had actually heard me. Man, God is real. He knows me. He hears me.

He answered me.   Me! He answered me! I would tell Mama that this was one she would definitely have to write in her little book.   This one she could put my name on cause today, God made Himself known to me again.

Chapter 7

That Brown Paper Bag

Some folks in the Black community still held that brown paper bag up as a measuring tape. If you were lighter than the bag, then you good. If you were darker than the bag, then it wasn't so good for you. The whole thing was stupid. It was awful. It was racist. Bad enough that we had to deal with racism out in the world but it is terribly sad that we have to deal with it where we are supposed to be safe, where we live; where we love. We still deal with racism among our own kind, every single day.

I often think that this hate was pressed down into our deepest memories during the God forsaking rides from the motherland in the hulking caverns of the slave ships that delivered us to hundreds of years of bondage. This demonic rotten seed was beaten and branded deep into our souls by the slave masters, overseers and by our own selves.

It was hammered into our heads as we were held in "our place" during the Jim Crow era. It was burned into our psyche with every cross lit by cowards hiding behind white sheets. It was scared into our hearts with every man, woman and child that was lynched, brutalized and murdered just because of the color of our skin. It was enforced and re-enforced, every time we were sent to sit at the back of the bus, to drink from separate fountains, to enter only from the back doors during the civil rights era. It was reminded by the denial of our votes at every ballot box that only allowed other races but not us.

Pitiful that we can't embrace the rich shades, the deep hues and every beautiful bit of black that we see. Why can't we know that to dislike the color of another's skin is to hate ourselves and to more importantly; hate God? God made us all, in His image. We are all His children. We are all pieces of God, just as our children are all pieces of us. God is love not hate. Hating us meant hating the very source that we came from. If only people could see that hating one another means that they just might be hating God.

Sad to say but some folks were religious about that bag and it was not going anywhere no time soon. Was a whole bunch of sad, but it was for real. Even though they didn't pull out the bag and put it against your skin, anymore; they still pictured it with their minds. Racism is a foul, ugly, dirty, stinky spirit that permeates our lives, our cores, our[1] minds and our hearts. I wished many times that they would put that bag on their heads to hide some of that filthy ugliness. If truth be told, those bags should have started a bond fire and sent all this self-hate right back to hell from where it came. Yeah; it was heartbreakingly sad. It was the truth of all truth that lie beneath the melatonin that God gifted us with.

God forgive them cause they definitely didn't know what they did. The bag was another chain constructed to keep our people in bondage. Pitiful that the chain was now welded by the very ones still in bonds, themselves. Others didn't have to work as hard to hold folks down cause we do a pretty good job of doing it all by ourselves. Most people would deny and never acknowledge the discrimination within that was still prevalent from the very community that was supposed to be our own. They did not see the pain, heartbreak and tears that the racism still reeked in our people. If only the could feel the pain, the isolation and the walls that the bag built. Lord knows somebody should have burned the bag long, long, long ago.

I was looking at the very proof that God heard me. God heard me. He really did. My first born looked white as any white baby when she was born. If I hadn't had her at home in my Mama and Daddy's bed, I might have thought that I had the wrong baby. Nobody in a hospital would have been able to convince me that she came out of me; except that I saw it for myself with my own two eyes.

I would have had some real serious questions about the baby that was in my Mama's hands if I hadn't been looking when that blond hair was coming out of me. I know me and I know that if I wasn't in total shock, they would have probably had me in a straight jacket fast, quick and in a hurry. Man, I would have been tearing up the whole place looking for my real baby if I had not seen her born.

I barely had any voice left from yelling and screaming during those labor pains. I was screaming my head off but I had both eyes wide open and was totally looking when she came out of me. Yes, the fact of things is, she really was mine. She was ours. God gave her to us. God gave her to Mama and me.

Chapter 8

A Girl Is Born!

My Mama was praying loud and hard as she caught that little girl when she entered this world. I teased her all the time that she was saved from birth. Y'all I promise you, the way my Mama was praying, that baby was saved, sanctified, filled with the Holy Ghost and could cry in tongues.

Lord knows, if my insides were not being ripped out, and my private parts were being ripped apart; I probably would have been laughing my head off at how seriously Mama was praying. The Father, Son, Holy Ghost and all of God's angels had been commanded to that room. If somebody else was in trouble right then, they was going to have to wait. Cause my Mama had all of the Help of Heaven in that room with me birthing that girl child.

Every since I can remember myself, I had teased about the way my Mama prayed. But Lord knows I would not have it any other way. Praying was as serious as life and death for Mama. Those prayers got us through when we had no clue. Those prayers lifted us from our lowest points when we could not see a way out. Those prayers also gave praise for every lesson, every good thing and every blessing. Those prayers saved us, watched over us, kept us. Those prayers opened doors that no man could close. They also put hedges of protection all around us. All I know in my heart is that I was probably never teasing ever again after this day. "Mama please, please, please. Never ever stop praying."

My Mama stared and grinned at that tiny bit of baby like someone gave her frankincense, incense and myrrh. Well these days, diamonds, silver and gold! I wanted to say, "Mama, it's just a little bit of baby." But I couldn't be the cause of taking away all of that joy that was flooding her face and heart.

We savored any joy we got a hold of. Cause joy came but it went again, way too fast. Fact is it always took its sweet time coming to visit. I was sure that I was going to bust as I sat watching my Mama savor all of this sweetness. The bundle that she held so reverently, amazed me. Cause this little bit of happy, I gave it to her. This bit of wonder, I birthed.

Man, when I think it through, we didn't get mega happy like this everyday. Our super joys were times that we held onto with both hands and feet. Those moments were not only special, they were extremely cherished and extraordinarily treasured. Those sweet bits of happy were guarded like the royals, the superstars or the presidents. Those were the times that got us through when things got bad. And bad times did come far too often.

Bad seemed powerful and impenetrable. Bad was in charge way too often. Ain't no doubt about it, bad plagued people like us. Bad came, went and came again. Slithered right in like a evil, slippery viper waiting to reek havoc in our already chaotic lives. And no matter how we tried to chop its head off, that snake would slither away rattling like it was laughing at us.

We just dealt with bad like an old unwelcome, uninvited guest that kept coming back no matter how hard we tried to lock the doors and windows. We ain't even looking at all the paper stuck in every crack and crevice trying to block the way. Somehow bad just kept getting in. Sometimes bad even acted like we were the intruders. On many occasions, I wondered if bad would lock us out in the blistering or freezing elements. Bad definitely acted like it owned the place, lock, stock and barrel.

No matter what, bad kept sneaking right on in. Bad was a greedy, mean, ugly, unwanted regular at the water pump and in our precious dinner pot. Bad jumped the line all the time, like it had priority over our thirsty throats and hungry bellies. Bad was so normal and so a part of our lives that it was almost strange for bad to be gone too long. Heck if bad was missing for a while, they would have probably sent out a search party like they were looking for a less than loved, but a familiar member of the house that had gone missing.

We believed and lived by the creed that 'we don't leave nobody out in the cold or the heat'. Guess that included bad too cause when bad knocked, somebody always opened the door, window or crack and ushered bad back in.

No matter how often bad came or how long bad stayed; bad ain't never stopped us from keeping on though. Good times always sent bad to the room like a misbehaving child when company visited. Sad thing is that as soon as company was heading to the door to leave, bad would slink back out and warm itself by the wood stove like a truant child that was finally free from punishment.

We didn't waste nothing in this life. Not one single thing was left out to be trashed. Y'all know the old folks used to say, "We use it from the rooter to the tooter!" They were talking about pigs and butchering but they meant it in every part of our lives. So we knew that we better wring every single second from this happy like the water that we wrung out of the clothes on wash day. We squeezed every single drop of happy when we got a chance and held on to it until the second that it was all gone.

When I think about it, I guess I really did give her something pretty important. I couldn't tear my eyes away from them. I gave my Mama her first grandchild, her future, her legacy, her love. She sure held her like she was a real and true miracle. Mama was crying, laughing and smiling. This moment really reminded me of those summer days when it was raining and the sun was shining.

Softly and reverently, she thanked the Lord for this tiny baby girl, anointed her with prayer oil, gave her back to God for His Glory, wrapped her in a handmade, soft blanket, then with tears streaming down her face, she stood holding her out to me. I just stared but I didn't raise my hands to take her. She stood waiting to hand that little girl to me and Lord knows if I could have I would have – run.

I had held a lot of babies in my life. I had 9 brothers and sisters that were all younger than me. Not to mention all of the family churn and the tons of bae-bae baddies that lived in the neighborhood. We always had a house full. Never lacked people asking me to look after churn while they tried to scratch and claw a living from any place that they could. I had been watching churn as long as I knew myself. But looking at that little thing in my Mama's hands made everything move in slow motion.

God almighty! Jesus, son of God! Lord have mercy, this was different. This was absolutely, positively; not the same. This was my baby! This was somebody that I had brought into this crazy old world. This was someone that I was expected to love, protect, teach, take care of and raise. Mercy God! I was not sure that I could do this. I was pretty sure that I couldn't do this. Lord a-mercy!

This was a real person. Every day this little person was going to need me. I would need to feed, clothe and shelter her. I would need to guide her, advise her and help her.

This whole little person would always look to me, to me, to me.... Father God! Holy Spirit! Lord Jesus what was y'all thinking up there giving me a real baby to take care of. As the old biddies was famous for saying, "What in heaven's name???"

My Mama must have known that all of these crazy thoughts was running through my head, a hundred miles an hour. No I'm sure that they were moving a thousand miles per hour. I could not move, think or pick my hands up to receive this little one.

I'm sure that my eyes were fluttering as fast as my heart and my breath. My lips were moving but I couldn't hear a thing coming out. Everybody in that room was looking at me. They were looking and waiting. I only heard my breath in my ears but it sounded like a loud rushing wind during the worst of storms.

Mama knew me better than I knew me, that's for sure. She knew that I was scared to death. I couldn't move, speak or hardly breathe. This was way too much. I was wondering if I was having a heart attack or maybe I was stroking out. I was stuck as stuck could be. Frozen solid like the ice blocks that they deliver on special occasions.

Mama expected more of me than I thought I had in me. Maybe she was confused about the person who she thought I was. I was truly doubting who I thought I was before this moment.

But God love her, Mama just stood there though and stared me down. She would not look away. I wanted her to give up and go away. So I tried to act like I was falling asleep. I closed my eyes tight. When I think about it now, I probably closed them way too tight. Ain't nobody could sleep with their eyes scrunched closed that tight. I counted to 100 all nice and slow. Then I slowly peeped out of one eye.

Lordy, Lord. My Mama was standing right there looking dead shot at me. Guess I hadn't fooled her any. That had worked so many times before. Maybe or maybe not, since it hadn't worked this time. Just maybe she had let me get away with it back then.

But not this time. Faking sleep was not going to work today, that's for sure. I had tried my level best. Today my best was certainly not good enough. Well now I figured I could mark acting off of my adult work list. Ain't no Oscar or Toni or none of them other awards in the future for me.

Mama hadn't moved a muscle. Not one single muscle. She was standing right there looking right at me. Oh Lordy, Lordy, Lord. Mama was not letting me get away with this. She was holding my feet to the fire.

She hadn't taken her hands away with that soft blanket draping her arms. I was gasping for air. Now I know that I was close to hyperventilating. Didn't seem like I could draw a deep enough breath to stop my chest from burning. My chest was going up and down like it was in a race for sprinters. My head was dizzy and I wasn't sure if I was going to faint or what. My eyes started twisting back and forth like I was at a tennis match.

What was I possibly thinking. Here I was looking for somewhere to run, an escape, a door, a bit of mercy. But there was not going to be any mercy, grace or escape for me. I had just birthed a baby. Ain't no running today. I could even think of standing up less more, running in the shape that I was in. My legs were still propped up in the air with the midwife pushing and massaging on my belly. She was humming and trying to soothe me, I'm sure. But all I could think of was running past all these church ladies as fast as I could and never coming back.

Nope running was not an option. It was time to pay the piper for those few minutes of rebellion in the backseat of that demon's car. Payday had come and I was the one that was here. So once again he was getting off Scott-free. Time was up. I had to pay up and grow up.

My Mama did not move and did not look away. Stood there with that tiny bundle held out, waiting for me. She didn't say a word, she just waited. And she didn't pull that bundle back to her chest, she held her hands out until I couldn't look away.

She was daring me not to be the woman that she raised me to be. She was calling that woman forth without a word. Her spirit was reaching out to mine. She was lifting me higher without touching me. She was walking me right into womanhood.

Mama eased down on the side of me, while never looking away. She didn't back up in the face of my fear. She didn't give me a pass or a get out of jail free. She was not letting me stay in the girl side of my existence. She was calling me up to another level. She was calling me to adulthood. She was demanding that I step into the woman in me. She was insisting that I be the Mother that she expected me to be. She was telling me to embrace this happy with her; but most importantly; with all of me.

Mama pushed back the covers down that I had unknowingly drawn up to my chin. She smiled, anointed my head, my hands and put that baby girl into my trembling arms. She didn't turn loose and she didn't move away. She kept her hands under my shaking ones, stabilizing all of us. She kept staring into my eyes with love and rock solid knowing.

Then I saw it. I saw and I believed. Deep down in my Mama's eyes, I saw all of it. I saw that it was alright. I could do this with God and my Mama holding us up. I was not alone.

Never would be. Praise Jesus, I would never have to do this by myself. I was not alone at all, with this thing. I never ever would be. I heard the humming of all those ladies who had been in this place before turn into joyous singing, whooping, shouting and praising as my baby girl let out a loud wail. Yes. Everything was better than fine. We; all of us, would raise this baby girl.

Chapter 9

An Old Soul

That baby girl opened those hazel eyes and I knew this was an "old soul" as the old people used to say. She looked at me just like she knew me. It seemed with that look she was making it clear that she knew all about me. I felt like she could see every part of me. She was looking at and touching my very soul.

I knew that she had already stole my Mama's heart and I was added to the list right then and there. She stared at me like she was waiting on me to talk to her. But I had no clue what to say because I already knew I was holding a wonder, a gift, a little piece of God. I could not believe that God Himself really trusted me to raise a baby. No, I was getting it wrong again. It was not just me. He trusted me, Mama and our village of love.

Thank goodness that I was never going to be a single parent. I was never going to have to do this by myself. No I had a whole love village to help me raise this little baby girl. Thank Goodness for that cause now that this baby entered the world and cried; things got real. It was not a fairytale anymore. The fantasy ended when she stuck her head out into the world.

The hen had come to roost. No Daddy for this baby cause the donor was running as hard and as fast as he could in every direction but mine. He was living his life with no thought of the life that he helped make. And he definitely was never going to be brave enough to come my way. That just might be the day, that I commit murder. So hopefully that day comes no time soon. Cause now that this baby was in my arms and not my belly, I was as serious as cancer. And we all know that cancer kills and I would too over this little one.

All we could depend on was God, Mama, me and our village. It was going to be what it was. We would just have to do the best we could. Just like always, just do the best we could. Prayerfully it would have to be enough. Enough to get her to be all that she could be. This moment cemented everything. This baby would be all that God intends.

My baby was smart from the moment she breathed. With some babies, you know right from the start. Mostly with those babies you can tell with certainty. They look at you like they completely understand every single word that you speak to them. They study you and stare like they wonder why you are doing the things you do. Then they give you the extra look that insinuates that you are not fooling them. They know the real deal.

So be advised that this is a watcher. Sometimes it is totally creepy when the baby is giving you that knowing look. How could this little thing that hasn't lived through anything yet be giving me that knowing look? They definitely make you rethink your actions when they are around and when they are not. I just automatically want to do the right thing cause I know that this baby will be watching.

From the very beginning my friends and family started looking at me crooked cause she was my Mama's as much as mine. I stayed with my Mama until she was almost 7 years old. What people looked at really strange was when I moved out, she stayed with my Mama.

I told her that I was going to move into my own house. She said that was cool. I said to her that she was moving too. She looked at me and shook her head no. With this one, that meant absolutely, positively, for real, for certain, no doubt- NO.

She was a very stubborn child. Once she made up her mind, it took earthquakes, tornadoes and avalanches to move her. I had learned this thing over the many head butting sessions between us.

One time, I was determined that she was going to eat what I fixed for breakfast. She was an extremely picky eater but I'm the Mom so I figured that she was going to eat or else. I made it clear that she wasn't leaving the table until that plate was empty. Those eyes turned bright and that lip set. I knew that the battle was on but I was stubborn too. Ain't that where she got it from?

Well everybody ate, scraped their plates, washed up and got on with the day. After the whole crew cleared out, one little button was still sitting at the table with a plate full. I cleaned up all of the dishes and looked at her occasionally daring her to sneak out. I decided to do some kitchen jobs that had been put off for a rainy day.

The sun was shining bright outside but a storm was brewing up in here. I cleaned all of the old food out the refrigerator, washed it down good and reorganized it painstakingly. Then I defrosted the freezer and put the like meats together. I emptied the ice trays into a bowl and refilled them. I cleaned all of the cabinets inside and out. My button was still sitting at the table with the food congealed, cold and looking at both of us. I kept going though. This little girl was not going to win this war.

Eventually I ran out of things to clean in the kitchen. I swept, mopped and waxed the floors. I prepared lunch and fed all of the kids and they ran on back to play in the neighborhood. She sat there with her full breakfast plate while the kids ate their lunch and waved at them when they were leaving.

I noticed some stuff was missing off of her plate when they left and I started to feel like I was getting some place. Then it hit me, my brothers and sisters probably felt sorry for her and sneaked some of the old food to help her. Oh no! They not fooling me none. That girl better believe that I was as stubborn as she was. Hell probably more. So I started cleaning on the already clean windows.

By the time I started on dinner I was getting a little bit worried. She hadn't eaten all day. Those old eggs had my spotless kitchen smelling. She refused to eat any kind of eggs. She hadn't drank anything either. The milk had not been touched the whole day. This kid hated milk but I kept trying cause she needed milk for strong bones right?

Well it wasn't long before Mama came from work. She came into the kitchen and greeted both of us as she took note of the ongoing war. She looked tired as all get out. She sat down at the table and I put a cold glass of lemon water and a sandwich cut in small pieces like she enjoyed it, in front of her. She crooked her finger towards the button bidding her to come get a snuggle on her lap.

She sipped her water and told me about her day. I noticed her letting the button sip from her glass. I refilled it and she kept talking. She put the button down, put a piece of sandwich in each hand and told her to gone outside cause we had some grown up talking to do. The button skipped right on out the back door and ran off to find the other churn. I started to say something but why bother cause my Mama had already called a truce and made this battle a draw.

I really can't be mad at her cause she won't leave my Mama. That girl followed my Mama from birth. She just move her eyes or head to wherever Mama was in a room. When she could see Mama, it kept her calm. If she was yelling her head off and Mama came in then that made everything alright. She would simmer down and look like she was asking, "Where have you been and what took you so long?" Lord knows if she heard Mama's voice then she wasn't satisfied until she was in her arms. Everything in her world was alright when Mama was rocking and humming.

Once she was crawling and walking, she was Mama's tiny shadow. Like she never wanted to be too far away from my Mama. I don't know, but I sure think that she shined a little bit brighter around my Mama. I ain't the least bit jealous either.

A lot of folks used to say that people like them were tied at the hip. I would always swear that they were tied at the heart. And believe it or not, that is really alright with me. Yeah, it's alrighty. See, I understood them perfectly; cause me and my Mama were tied up pretty tight too. We'd been tied up first and nobody but nobody was ever going to undo that. We'd be tied up til Jesus come. Now, then and forever.

I ain't jealous about Mama's closeness with this little girl, cause every good thing in me, my Mama put it there. So I already know that she will do the same for our baby girl. Yep, I said our. Mine and hers, all the way. We had made a deal when I was pregnant. Making a deal with Mama is in my mind like making a deal with God. No devil in hell or earth could ever cause her to break a promise. She would keep her word until the rapture comes.

Chapter 10

Meet Your Seed!

I know that babies with parents normally have a Mom and a Dad. But my baby has me and my Mama. The sperm donor saw her one time when she was almost five. She was out with my sister who was dating his cousin. While at the cousin's house he stopped by. Bet he was not expecting the surprise of his life; but there it was.

His aunts had always known my baby. They had been standing there in the room when she was born. They had always been a part of her life. They got regular pictures and visited constantly. Couldn't have a family gathering without them there. They'd been lifelong friends with Mama even before the visit to their nephew's backseat.

So when my little sister started dating one of the aunt's sons, they got to see even more of my baby. If they had not been family before, they were now.

The date that he met his seed; my sister said he acted like he was choking on a big fat seed. She told me that he turned red as red could be the minute he saw that little girl. He just stared and couldn't say nothing. That little girl was on the floor playing with the little box of toys his aunties kept in the closet for when she came over there. And all he could do was stare.

The toy box was constantly changing cause they were always adding some new toy or book that they knew she would love. Then of course they'd make sure she had a book to take home with her. The aunties knew that she loved books probably more than she even thought about toys. That itty-bitty girl-child was cherished from every direction.

As he stood in the doorway watching her read her new book out loud to the Aunties; no one had to tell him who she was. She was brighter skinned than him. She had reddish blond and brown hair. She got to the end of the paragraph without missing a single word and pronouncing each one distinctly. Then she broke into her brightest smile and those hazel eyes shined green as she waited for the Aunties' praises that always flowed abundantly and without fail. Except today they failed, they were staring at the man in the doorway while my baby girl was staring at them.

He was a disc jockey and a ready showman; so the shock didn't last too long. He hit his stride; fast, quick and in a hurry. He went up to my little girl, smiling, grinning and talking to her. As soon as my sister heard his voice, she ran as fast as she could. She looked terrified as she scooped up my daughters and got her away from him. She was fully aware that he had told people that I lied. But what made me sick still was that he had denied this child.

My sister gathered her things and was getting out of there as fast as humanly possible. As she slid by him, heading to the door, he put a dollar bill in my baby's hand. He asked my sister to wait so he could talk to her some more. He acted like seeing her had affected him. He acted like he was happy to see her. Well she was five years old; about time.

But my sister knew that I would kill her dead if she didn't get my baby out of there and home to me right away. She was scared to death of what I might do if I found out that he had seen and talked to my baby. All the way home in the car, she kept asking my girl not to talk about that man when she got home. She promised her everything as long as she did not mention that man.

Our girl had been reading since she was two. I gave her every book, magazine or paper with words on it that I could find. She couldn't get enough words. Ain't had no money to buy books cause we had to buy food. Made me feel real bad that I couldn't give her everything she needed. I just kept doing the best I could. I'd tear pages from magazines in the doctors office and any place that I saw magazines. Just so she could smile real big as she read the words out loud to me. Whenever I saw somebody giving away books, I made sure to get them for her.

So as soon as our baby girl made it into the house, she ran over and was showing Mama her new book that she had held onto during the quick exit. She opened the book and the dollar bill fell out on the floor. She squealed and hopped around in her excitement. She picked up the dollar and asked Mama could she go up the road to the candy lady's house.

Our neighbor sold penny candy and cookies to all of the neighborhood children and soda pop and beer to the adults. Every penny they got, they ran to the candy lady for a piece of candy or a cookie. She was itching to get there right now cause she had a whole dollar. That could mean 100 of something sweet. And this little girl loved everything sweet.

I was standing at the ironing board and asked her which auntie gave her a whole dollar. She usually came home with a quarter or two. Only during the holidays or birthdays did she come home with dollars. She held her dollar up and admired it in the sunlight streaming through my freshly washed windows as she told me that the Aunties did not give her this dollar.

She started twirling and spinning in her excitement as she told me all about the tall pretty man that gave her that dollar. She told me that my sister had made her leave the Aunties before they was ready for her to go home. She complained about not getting to get her snack that the aunties always had for her. But now she could buy some sweets and make that sweet tooth happy.

Everything in the house went quiet. Everything stopped except the bouncy excited girl that was waving a dollar and telling all of us about her visit. I noticed that nobody in the whole house was moving. Then my Mama stood up and blocked the doorway. If I could have put two thoughts together then I would have known that she was trying to keep me from going to hunt him down.

I put the iron down. Then I just stood there. I have no idea how much time went by. I was in shock. For the first time in five years he had seen the proof of what happened in the back seat. The proof that I had not lied. The proof that there was a five year old child in the world that he helped make and that he had done absolutely nothing for.

That tall pretty light skinned man could only have been the sperm donor. I moved like lightning and grabbed that dollar bill out of my girl's hands like it was on fire or a lethal poison. I put on my shoes, picked up my purse and moved quickly to the door. My Mama took a look and moved.

I had tunnel vision with everything rimmed in a red haziness. I could faintly hear my Mama calling my name. Later she told me that she had been screaming louder than she had ever screamed before or since. But I was barely registering her screaming. Or our girl who was screaming her head off cause she knew her penny candy and soda pop was going out the door in my hand.

All that screaming sounded like mere whispers. I had loud waves booming in my ears and my heart was beating out of my chest. I was probably having a heart attack the way my chest was squeezing and hurting. All I knew was before I stood in judgment before God, I was going to kill the donor for talking to my baby and for put a fricking dollar in her hand. A dollar for five years. The only thing that he had ever given her and it was one dollar.

I went straight to the Aunties house. Everybody there got out of my way real fast. The Red Sea could not have parted any smoother or faster. I know I was looking crazy cause I sure felt like it. I was falling head-first right off of the highest cliff and straight into crazy with a capital C. This fool had done absolutely nothing for me or my baby, ever. Now he decided that after five years; a dollar would pay his way into my girl's life.

He had the nerve to give my 5 year old girl; a dollar. A freaking dollar was all he put in her hands after five years. I guess he figured that dollar covered her food, clothes, medical bills and everything else that she had needed for five years. I guess he felt like a big man cause he had finally done something for her. Well he was getting his dollar back. The devil is a liar and he is one too.

I walked straight up to him. He had the nerve to smile and say my name. He started saying how beautiful and smart our daughter was. Our? Our? I clocked him dead in the mouth. I tried to knock all of his teeth out with one punch. I was going to stuff that dollar down his throat and pray that he choked on it. I wanted it so far down his gullet that Jesus would have to pull it out while he stood at the pearly gates waiting for judgement. I wonder how many people had died of choking on a dollar bill?

Luckily for him, it was in that moment that my Mama and all my brothers arrived. They tackled me and dragged me out of there. Some of the men at the Aunties' house had to help get me out. Saved his life is what they did. Tore up the Aunties house pretty good; getting me away from him. I kind of felt bad about that part. But I felt real good about knocking him in the mouth.

He had no clue how close he came to meeting Jesus up close and in person that day. I was determined to kill him dead. I know he probably thought that he could walk in and be "Daddy" after five long hard years. But he could go straight to hell. I was not going to stop until he has his ticket to get there. Nothing would make me feel better until they were driving him to church in the backseat of a hurst.

We ain't got to have the donor to raise this little girl. We could get this done. Ain't worrying about him and for real. I hoped and prayed that he would never enter my presence again in life after denying my baby and leaving me to deal with all of the mess by myself. I was a 17 year old teenager and he was a very grown man. Had no right messing with somebody my age anyway.

I was 17! Should have let my parents put that pitiful excuse of a man in jail for statutory rape. He better be real glad that we just didn't know about those laws back then. I sure would have told my Mama and Daddy to get him locked up. I had no pity for him cause he had none for me and none for my baby. I just know that I would have prayed for them to throw away the key.

But no luck, he thought he got away free and clear. But what he got was missing out. He missed those sweet smiles. He missed those tiny arms hugging your neck.

He missed her firsts – teeth, walking and talking. But just know and believe, it's all good. Mama and me are like good coffee on a cold winter day; strong, warm, sweet and black. No worries, We got this!

No since showing up now. After all this time; he finally wanted to come clean about that night. That low-down, no good. whoring, halfbreed, pretty boy, Disc Jockey that I slept with only one time; ran. Man! Yep! pregnant after one time.

They say it can't happen. But I am proof cause it sure did. It happened to me. That Nig... ok I'm not supposed to say that word but y'all know I'm thinking it and drooling to say it! But I am going to respect my Mama, definitely not that nig... I couldn't help it. All those promises before the back seat and all of the lies afterwards.

Okay I guest I need to say why I hate the very air he breathes, the ground he walks on and the half white skin he lives in. If he was on fire, I would not spit on him. Yes sir-ree, I would let him burn. I would probably throw gas on him to make sure it was a huge bond fire. A cotton picking barn burner that wouldn't go out for days! Yeah,

I'd make sure that there was plenty of gas on the ready cause I sure wouldn't want the fire to die down too soon.

My Mama tried to talk to me about not hating him my whole pregnancy. She tried everything. Even told me that my baby was going to look just like him if I didn't stop hating him. Well that didn't work cause I had thought he was cute enough before we did the do. She tried to "God" me into forgiving him but the Lord knows my heart and that ain't happening no time soon; if ever.

No ma'am. I won't hate him cause I sure ain't going to hell cause of him. Well maybe a little hate wouldn't hurt. But you best believe your first, last, top and bottom dollar, that I don't like him. Yeah Lord, all love is totally lost.

Y'all have to believe me. I'm not a bad person. I'm really not. See, he did the ultimate sin in my book. My book was big, real big; cause I was not trying to forget all this wrong stuff that had been done to me and around me all my life. So I kept notes and tried hard not to forget.

Old people said don't forget history cause then you'd do it all over again. What he did was probably pretty wrong in the book of every 17 year old girl with a belly that now was trying to blow up real fast after a few minutes in the back seat of an old car with a irresponsible loser that was only after one thing. Then he was in the wind.

My whole life totally changed after those few minutes. But he just went right on without a thought or backwards glance at me or the baby "we" made. Yeah, Pretty Boy, just kept right on living and screwing every Tina, Deb and Hatty that his eyes landed on. Every girl around fell at the feet of that pretty boy. Guess I could not be too mad. I fell by choice. No body had forced me to get in that backseat.

It just made me crazy that he did not even think about how this baby, that he helped make, was going to eat, live and grow up with nobody but me. He did not think about this little girl growing up without a Daddy; without him. He did not think about his actions changing lives; his, mine, my Mama's and this sweet little baby girl's, forever and ever.

No he was a selfish fool! Yeah, he was all about him. To me, he is, was and was always going to be the lowest of the low. He had all the fun but refused to pay the piper or the child support. That's alright though cause you can run but you can't hide . Yep them old people again, always said if you play, payday is coming after while, believe that.

See I could have moved on and never shed a tear over him but he didn't just hurt me. He had hurt an innocent newborn baby that didn't ask to be here. We did that. We decided to have a few minutes of unprotected sex and a whole lot of people was going to pay the price for it. Yeah, the lowdown denied me but more so, he denied my baby. All that means is that me and Mama would raise her best we can. Together we can do it, Yep and we can and will do it real good. So he can just watch our smoke.

I know one thing, he better not show up trying to take credit for something that he refused to do. He better not come around trying to play Daddy after we did all of the work. He deny her now, then we will deny him later. I just hope he don't make me kill him. Cause I know I would be happy to kill him dead if he ever approached my girl again. He ran then, so he could just keep it moving. Move right on out of our lives.

Chapter 11

<u>Moving On...</u>

I never thought I was smart with books. I stopped school in high school cause I was watching the babies at home while Mama went to work. She spent all day cleaning white folks houses for pennies. We really needed the money cause Daddy worked all week but got drunk on Friday when the workday was done. He drank up a bunch of the money not thinking about all of those hungry churn at the house. They had lots of babies too cause ain't nobody was passing out birth control back then, especially in our neighborhood. Shucks! Don't get me started on all that stuff

When Mama could not take all those drunken weekends with no money for the next week anymore; we moved. Daddy went to work and we had family and friends show up with trucks. We could do bad all by ourselves and not have to deal with a drunk. Mama and I were going to raise the rest of the churn together.

We got moved in and started making things work. We were a good team. Actually we were an amazingly great team. Mama worked and I took care of the house, meals, cleaning and the churn. We ran a tight ship. Just kept praying away storms that might throw us off course. Did not need anything or anyone sinking our ship.

Life kept on going and I kept right on living. I kept trying to find love but instead I found zeros. I thought if I stayed away from those light skinned pretty boys that I might have better luck. Wanted to see another side of life, so I got with that old saying, "The darker the berry, the sweeter the juice." Only the berries that I found were definitely sour.

Those dark guys didn't work out for me either. I had three more baby girls by guys that were gone before my babies crawled across the floors. It really didn't matter if those sperm donors were out of my girls' lives. Those men were the ones missing out on the sweet hugs, the sticky kisses, the kiddie knowledge and the scraped knees. They did not know that I had gifts from God Himself. I had sweet little angels in my hands while they all continued to be cowards. They just went right on running to the next pair of open legs while I raised their kids.

I could not quit. I had four girls to raise and hopefully they would do better than me in the relationship department when they grew up. I would just remind them of all of my mistakes. Hopefully they would learn from them and never ever repeat them. I did not want my girls figuring that they could not live without men. They absolutely could.

I just kept my head up and kept it going. It was hard but I kept believing while I raised four girls with the help of God, my family and our village. No fathers in the picture but I couldn't give up. Those four girls were depending on me. I would give everything for them but I sure wished that I could have a little something for myself too.

I guess every place I went I kept looking. I spent so much time looking. Looking for what? I was out there looking for love. Guess I just never stopped looking in the wrong places. Love was an elusive thing that I never found in the arms of a man. But that didn't stop me from looking every single day of my life for it.

I laid in a lot of arms but none of them loved me like I wanted or deserved to be loved. None of them loved me like God and the Bible said I was supposed to be loved.

Even though I was trying, it was so very hard and I was getting tired of looking. That old sweet fairytale was still playing in the back of my mind and my heart was beating to the rhythm of happily ever after. So I kept going and kept looking.

I looked in the stores. I looked at church. I looked at family gatherings. I looked at dances, clubs, sports games, butcherings, harvestings and community affairs. The problem was it wasn't too many men looking back. In this little old town it was extremely scarce pickings.

I wished. I pleaded. I imagined. I even bargained with the Man upstairs. Pretty sure that He wasn't listening real good on that one. I prayed and asked God for some eligible single handsome young men that would move here. Hell I wasn't greedy, I told God if He would listen one more time that I would really appreciate it. "Father God, please just send one. One for me."

After I found the right one and we fell in love, we could move away. My sister had married the donor's cousin and they were living all the way in Washington DC. Another one of my little sisters married a young man and they were living in Columbus, Ohio. A third younger sister married and was living in the suburbs of Charleston. Lord, when is it going to be my turn? I'm the oldest. The firstborn girl so where was my husband? Didn't seem right but all three of my younger sisters were married and settled down. They had homes, husbands and were working on families. And here I was single with four little girls with no Daddies to be known, seen, or found.

My life sure didn't have no knights in shining armor. Couldn't buy, borrow or steal a white picket fence. I know things could be worse but they wouldn't be getting better until a little bit of love came my way. I ain't going to give up.

I was believing for someone to finally see that I am wife material. The Bible says, He who finds a wife, finds a good thing. I am a good thing. I am willing to spend my life proving it. Guess I will just have to keep looking until he finds me. Keep looking until I find someone of my own to love me. Someone that chooses to stay with me. One thing that I do know is if they choose me, I'd stick and stay no matter what. I wouldn't dare go away. Bet that!

Chapter 12

Churn Know!

I should have paid attention to my oldest girl. The old people always used to say that churn and animals know when somebody is bad. They just know. Seems like they can smell it all the way to the bone. Can't hide that putrid evil spirit from the pure and innocent. They just know. Watch how they take or don't take to somebody. Pay real close attention and that will tell you if you need to run. If they ain't buying then you'd better not either. When they run one way, you'd better be running too. No questions. No statements. No comments. Just run.

But once again I was not listening. I didn't want to hear it. I refused to listen to anything negative about him. I wasn't paying attention. Every time somebody tried to get me to listen or see; I looked the other way or covered my ears real tight. I was willing to let nothing or nobody mess this up for me. It was finally my chance and I was not going to waste it. I was in the front of the line and I was not going to let anybody cut in front of me. No! Not this time. I was getting mine!

I was just so lonely. I was lonely through and through. Lonesome as the cowboys on the range in those old western songs. Lord knows I was not telling people about it but it was always right there. I breathed lonely in and blew lonely out. All I know is it coated my mouth with a nasty sick bitter taste. It oozed down my throat like that old stinky castor oil that they used to give us every year with the excuses that it was killing bugs, worms and germs. It roiled and bubbled in my belly like old bad spoiled rotten food. It was on my skin like a thick coat of Petroleum jelly that they rubbed us up with before sending us out to face the coldest winter weather.

I was lonely in places that I didn't know I had. Jesus! I was so lonely that my heart ached as lonely slid, creeped and oozed into every crack and crevice. I thought and felt like I was in physical pain all the time. Ain't no aspirin could help this. No hospital could cure this sickness. I was in critical condition. Lonely was my terminal disease but I wanted to live.

It felt like lonely was choking the life outta me. I'd lived through some things so I wasn't going to just lay down and die. I was going to fight for me, fight for happy, fight for love. I figured out fast that getting real with me;

wasn't easy. I truthfully do know that lonely was all in my mind.

I was surrounded by people constantly. Could hardly breathe or take a pee by myself. If I was being honest, that didn't make it hurt any less. I think if I was gonna tell the truth; I would say I was in pain all day, every day. I felt like it hurt worse than anything if I had to measure this pain called lonely.

I was raising the churn while Mama worked. I kept everybody fed, bathed, clean and out of trouble. I helped with all of the neighborhood churn while people tried to work. I figured I was doing my part. I was helping all I could. I just needed some help for me too. I kept Mama's house and mine spotless. I made dinner for her house and others in the neighborhood every week day.

I directed yard work and made sure the garden was tended. I was willing to take whatever stress or bother that I could off of my Mama. I wanted to make her life a little easier cause she worked so hard. I worked hard too. My uncles used to tease that I outworked 3 women and two men on my slow day. I did my best not to let them be called liars either.

I just wanted a little something for me. I wanted my fairytale too. I wanted what everybody else seemed to get so easy. Some girls fell in and out of love as often as they changed their panties. I just kept getting close but then everything fell apart and I was going back to the end of the line. I deserved some happy. Lordy, Lordy! I was just so tired of not having anybody for me. I really wanted somebody to love. The Lord knows you heart. God knows me! I just wanted somebody to love me.

I didn't pay no attention to our girl when I brought that short dark smooth talking man home to my Mama's house. I told my girl to come say hi. She took one look, those funny colored eyes got big as marbles and turned bright green. Off she ran to my Mama as fast as those legs could go. I didn't understand it at all.

She was a friendly little thing. Talked to everybody about everything. But she had no words for my new man. She just kept peeping from around Mama. But she never came back. And shockingly, she never said another word the whole time that he was there. She was always talking so I was amazed that she was acting like this. She usually had so much to say. People met her and was always surprised at her fast mouth and her quick mind.

Our girl didn't meet strangers. So it was really weird that she utterly and totally refused to come back. I kept calling her but she was cemented to my Mama's hip. She wouldn't even look my way.

Good thing company was in the house cause I would have jerked that little girl off of her feet if she didn't answer or come when I called. I tolerated no disobedience, disrespect or discussion from children. So I guess I was on my best behavior too, cause I just called her occasionally and tried to give her the eye but she acted like she didn't see and didn't want to hear me. She stayed far away.

What was going on that little Miss Friendly herself totally and irrefutably refused to say anything to him or to come near him; was blowing my mind. It should have been a big red flag and a bright blinding light. But I had a man. A man of my very own, so I didn't care cause I figured that she would warm up to him and us later. Oh my God! I was finally a US!

My guy tried over and over. He went above and beyond. It was hard for him too. He was used to his charm luring women of all ages into his fan club. Those he couldn't charm, he tried to buy. He tried candy, gum and even a dollar. But that girl was not having none of it and none of him.

A dollar was a lot, these days. She could have bought 100 pieces of gum, cookies or candy from the old lady down the street that sold sweets at her back door. But she left that dollar on the table and refused to take it even after he left. Still I blew it all off. I wish that I could have paid attention to my child instead of that fake charmer cause he was a snake in disguise. I just couldn't see it then. I didn't want to see it.

I should have taken note but my mind was on cloud nine. Floating high above everything around me. My feet hadn't touched the ground since I met him. He had made it clear to every single person that he was interested in me and only me. This wasn't like me. This whole thing was new and I was loving every bit of it.

True enough that I didn't want it to stop, go away or end. Just having my own man that was staying on, was something I just wasn't used to either. Couldn't pay me to pay attention to nothing but him. My mind was completely blown. I woke up with him on my mind. Thought of him all day. Went to sleep with him on my mind. All I wanted to see, smell, taste, touch or hear was him. My head was turned by everything sweet that he was whispering in my ears. The sad thing is, I was so happy that somebody was finally whispering that I never wanted it to stop.

I just wanted to pitch my tent right there in fairyland. Hell, I wanted to brick it in. Build a fort and add a moat. Put some cannons on the wall in every direction for intruders that came to disturb my happiness. Didn't want nobody or nothing to move me from this place.

Chapter 13
Real Enough?

I know it was not real but for now, it was real enough. Most times wants just don't outweigh the truth. Good things do come to an end, weather we want them too or not. No matter how hard or long we try, we can't stop the inevitable. Doesn't matter how we kick, stream, holler or fight. It is what it is. Eventually the truth will seep into fantasyland. The sun will shine into the darkness. Reality will raise it's ugly head and ain't nothing we can do about it.

Even from the beginning, that unwanted ending was always looming in my peripheral. When it tried to move into my line of sight, I'd turn my head, look away or close my eyes. It became a nervous habit for me to close and squeeze my eyes and hands, tight. I'd squeeze them so tight that I'd give myself a headache.

Many times I would wonder why my face was hurting and I'd realize that I was causing it by clenching my teeth and jaws with all my might. Then I realized that I was holding my entire body tight as a rubber band. Guess I figured if

I clenched down with everything that I have then I might get somebody just for me.

I wanted to hold on to him, keep him, love him. But once again I could hear the truth whispering into my covered ears, reminding me that rubber bands can only stretch so far or so many times. Then they pop. Rubber bands are flimsy, brittle, temporary and made not to last. Just like this relationship... temporary.

But my life was already factual. I already knew, fairy tales are not real and they definitely don't last forever. What I didn't know, a ton of people around me kept telling me. I didn't want to hear it. I didn't want to see it. I didn't want to know it. I refused to give up the one thing I wanted, dreamed of, needed.

I just wanted to hold onto my little bit of happy for a little while. If I was being honest, I wanted to hold on for as long as I possibly could. I wanted to squeeze every drop of happy out of this relationship before the good times ended. Yes, even as it began, I already knew that there was an ending. I was just hoping and praying that it was a happy one.

Our girl wouldn't have none of him no matter how hard he tried. She was stiff and clenched as tight as me, when he came around. She acted scared of him like he was the devil himself. I didn't know what people were saying that she had heard but I was not going to let them ruin this through my girl. I talked to her every time I saw her and told her how much he loved her and how much he loved me. She could see that I was happy.

I was not sitting around sad and brooding since he came. I know that it was bad of me to hope that a little girl would see how bad I wanted this and not do anything to end it for me. I already knew that I would be expected to choose my girls over a man. I just didn't know if I was strong enough to do the right thing. I had wanted this for so long that I wasn't willing to let anyone get in the way; even my own babies.

I would do whatever it takes to make this right for everybody. I would just try harder to get my girls to love him like I did. I would show them that he was going to be nice to me and to them. Then they'd see what a good thing this was for them but most of all, how good it was for me.

My guy was determined to sway my girl. He went out of the way to friend her. She wasn't having it, no matter how hard he tried. He never saw her without sweets, quarters, gum or gifts. He always had something for her. He made sure to slip little things in her hand that he gave no one else but her. If she mentioned a treat, he bought it. If she wanted to go for a ride, we all piled into the car cause then he felt like going for a ride.

He would not tell her no and didn't want me to either. Even when he told me no, she could change his mind. It was bad of me but sometimes when I wanted stuff, I would ask her if that is what she wanted; so she'd ask him. Once she got to asking, he made it happen. I didn't even see that as bad. I should have but I didn't want to. I just wanted to hold on to any bit of happiness I could get. Even if I was using my child to get a bit of happy, that didn't stop me from clutching those good moments.

I don't know why I didn't pay attention. Okay, I do know but I didn't want to know. I just wanted to keep my fake fairytale going. Even though I already suspected, no; I always knew exactly how fast it could turn into a nightmare. I just wanted to keep dreaming. Even when the nightmare raised its ugly head, I was quick to knock it down as soon as possible and run as fast as I could right back to fake-fairyland. I wasn't leaving here, no matter what. I was willing to settle for the dream. Fake and all. It was so nice and happy there. Happy was good even if it was faked happy.

I didn't want to face the facts cause then it would be time to see me. I have to live with all of me including the me that only I see. I was trying my best to be the best me I could be. I wanted to be proud of me. I wanted to love me. Hell, I would settle for just liking me.

I know that the time was here to face me. Time to see me for who I truly was. Time to see all of me. I needed to be able to look myself in the eye and know that I was not hiding a thing. I wasn't sure if I was ready or able to do that. I could not afford to hate myself and expect everybody else to love me. Love started right here with me being straight with me. It is easy to lie to others but I can't lie to me. I want to deserve respect so I have to respect me first.

I would have to face the real me. The me that only I see. The me that nobody else knows but a few that have touched my heart and soul. A few that I let in to know the true me. Those that love me in spite of. I want them to know that loving me is a good thing. I don't want to waste their time and especially not their love. I know nothing is easy in this world but I keep trying to make me better each and every day. I want the me I am to be the me that my Mama loves. I know that there are many people that I can fool about who I am, but I can't fool me. So I'm done with that.

When I looked into my heart and soul, I didn't like the me that I was seeing. The me that was scared, lonely, hurt, tired, fat, just cute not pretty, not beautiful, not successful, losing constantly, less than, drowning, never getting on top, discouraged, disappointed, depressed, sad and mad as hell. The me that knew all of the secrets and couldn't hide them cause I was refusing to look. Lord knows, that was a lot. More than I ever wanted to face or admit to.

No! That part of me I stayed far far away from all that, whenever possible. Who the hell wanted to see all of that? Not me, that's for sure. I kept that door locked up good and tight. Even thought a time or two about throwing away the key. Cause Man, that's way too much stuff for anybody. At least it was way too much for me.

114

And ain't nobody want to sit around with all that, every day and every night. No siree, I sure didn't want to visit with me too often. Nobody I ever met, heard of or that I could think of, wanted any of that. I would stick with happy. That's what I was going to do.

Chapter 14
<u>Old Sayings</u>

Some people are so superstitious. They swear by the old wives tales, fables, sayings, myths, legends and stories. I always thought that most of it was foolishness but all of it is based on some sort of truth; if only a thin thread. It hurt my heart sometimes when those old sayings stabbed the me that I tried to keep hidden and safe.

Those truths slid under the door into all of my favorite hiding places. They were razor blade sharp so they cut and sliced with the precision of a surgeon's scalpel. They rooted out the lies that I tried to tell me. They exposed the fallacies that I told me to embrace. They drilled off every lock that was supposed to protect me. Why didn't they just go away and leave me be?

I knew that even though some things don't feel good, they can be good. Words can be like medicine. So I just took to heart what I liked and threw the rest of life's lessons right under my high heels. These fat flat feet weren't made for walking but I kept it moving. Yes ma'am, I moved right on with a smile on my lips, a twist of my hips and a swagger in my step; just like I owned every single thing that I faced.

Too bad, I didn't own much of nothing. Them old gossips that watched my every move; would have been quick to say that, "I didn't have a pot to piss in or a window to throw it out of." Old hags! I had pots, might be rusty, missing a handle or two and some even had leaks; but they were my pots. My windows were missing some panes, a few were boarded up and others were painted shut too. I was just glad that I had some pots and some windows. Those old bitties didn't need to know all that stuff though. They would have shook their heads, crossed their arms, tsked tsked and looked on while giving me the evil eye.

I hugged those old wives tales so hard some days, that they almost choked the life out of me. All I know is that I really didn't need all that truth slapping me up side the head. I told me that too much ain't good for nobody. Best not to look too close. Definitely ain't trying to listen either. I was determined to stay in the fight. So gossip and gossipers or not; I encouraged myself. "Head up, Sister-Girl. Lady first, then the rest. Keep it moving, Honey-Child.

Yep, Cover that mirror up Chic! Just do like they do when somebody dies in the family and it's time for the wake. Every mirror and shiny thing got covered, preferably covered in black to let you know death was in the house. Don't want you to look in the mirror and see death, spirits, demons or any evil things coming for you.

The mirror I kept covered looked into my face, my heart, my mind and my very soul. That mirror was definitely staying covered. I was willing to fight the devil himself to make sure that nobody ever removed those covers. Nope definitely refused or wanted to see all of that old stuff. I was taking a hard pass on that play.

Chapter 15
My Man?

There are some things that are extremely hard to admit, even to me. It's hard, sad and devastating but in the cold hard light of day, it's true. What is really bad about this whole situation is, that this short, ugly, mean, selfish, demonic little man was not even all that.

He wasn't even my type if truth be told. Even with the lack of men, I did have a type. That scalpel was cutting again cause I liked them light, bright, smart, tall, good looking and full of muscles; just like my oldest girl's sperm donor. But because the donor had done me bad and had denied my baby; I denied myself of my desired type. I stayed far away from those pretty men.

Proof of that was sleeping in my bed every night. He was Lazy with a capital L, short, black as night and f-ugly, man. Wondering what f-ugly is? It so ugly that you had to add another letter so they could come to the front of the line and get a triple helping.

And Lord let's not forget po. Just Po cause he could not afford the other "o" or the "r" to make poor. Geez he was also skinny. People used to say that he was as skinny as I was fat. Some would probably have said, "as skinny as skinny could be; in the body and the pocket". What a pair we made. Him skinny as a bean pole and me as big as a house. Fool that I was, I just figured that I would fatten him up, fix his clothes, his shoes, his hair, his skin, his pissy attitude and then keep him for myself. At least I had a man.

Ain't much I could do about lazy. This was the laziest man that I have ever seen. Here goes those old folks sayings again; "He wouldn't work in a pie factory if he was getting free pies." He hated to do any manual labor. Didn't know a hammer from a screwdriver. Couldn't tell the difference between a rake and a hoe. Could not drive a truck or a tractor. He hated being dirty so farming was out. Complained about working in the weather so construction was a no go. Couldn't boil water or crack a egg so cooking was not a possibility. Here I was settling for someone that couldn't keep a job and would never have a career. What was I thinking... I already know. I was not thinking.

Guess I was low on the esteem meter or just plain tired of waiting for somebody to love me. That no good, low down bastard had sworn that he loved me right from the start. He told everybody that it was love at first sight.   I thought he was nearsighted for sure. But anyway! He was screaming that he loved me before he knew my last name good. Sure could not spell it, that was for sure. Once again, I missed it.

All of that I love you on the first night we met, should have been a flashing, blinking, blinding, neon sign; but we already know, I ain't no good with signs. Got me plenty blind spots where those signs are concerned. If folks got to looking, they just might find that I got a hidden suitcase full of tickets cause I'm so bad with those cotton picking old signs. It didn't matter, Stop, yield, curve, intersection, detour or any of the rest. Not one of them signs ever really worked for me. That's for sure!

I know for sure, I ain't no psychic cause I ain't so good at seeing the future. Hell I didn't want to look at the present so I know that I was not in a rush to see that freight train of hurt and pain coming down the track heading straight for me. That train was chugging away with the whistle blowing at full volume trying to warn me. But just like I would not look at the signs, I covered my ears every time I heard the hint of a whistle.

The wheels were rusty and the train was older than the lies my Daddy tried to tell on payday when the whiskey was tall and the money was short. Should have heard and seen it a mile away. Nope not me though. I was determined to let the dice fall where they may; even to my own destruction.

I really truly prayerfully was hoping that just maybe the pain train was heading somewhere else or aiming at somebody else. But no! It was a locomotive with one route and one destination on the schedule – my life. Sadly, painfully, devastatingly that train would chug right along in and out of my life on a continuous loop.

I was so tired of looking that I just didn't want to see it for what it was. Keeping it real, a lot of it I didn't want to know. I refused to see whenever anybody got a peek at the real real. Didn't want to hear nothing bad about him or us. I just wanted love and I was willing to settle for any little bit that came my way.

Real life shaking, earth shattering Love is all that I wanted. What could possibly be wrong with that? But since that ain't never came my way, I was willing to settle for the mess I made it. Mess mixed with my little bit of love. I was willing to love him enough for the both of us. In my heart I recited the mantra that played in my head like a scratched record album, "Everybody deserves a tiny speck of love at least once."

I know me... I know us. Us who? All of the women in my family, that's who. Every single one of us, once we make up our minds, we love hard. We love with everything in us. We love like we done walked down the aisle with a dry old preacher reciting those age old marriage vows. Bad thing is didn't need a preacher to say it, we just did it.

We acted like it was ingrained into our very DNA. We acted like it was flowing through our veins. We are the type that will squeeze blood out of a turnip, even if it was blood that flowed out of our hands from doing all that wringing. No way, no when, no how. We don't ever stop loving. We don't quit when we love. We just don't give up on love. We love til death do us part. Yep! I loved him to death. Just wish I had known that it would be my death...

Chapter 16

Behind God's Back

The town I lived in was so tiny. So tiny that I bet some people in our own state would not even know where to find it. Don't even bother thinking people from other places would know that we are back here. But we definitely are right here. Of that, I am sure. Some used to joke that we were behind God's back and He couldn't even see us.

Most times I was in full agreement with that. I probably would have agreed all of the time, except now and then He peeked over His shoulder to remind us that He was still there. One thing for sure, the devil sure knew where we was. We tried hard to stay out of his sight but he did what ever he could to keep us in as many messes as possible. We hid when we had to. We showed up as necessary. We just kept it going.

Yes, here we are. If the Lord threw a rock at us it probably would not even know where to land to find us. It would most likely boomerang and hit him in the head. Okay I guess it is probably not good to make jokes about

God.   But living way out here in the boonies was a joke all in itself.

This poor little old town only had one flashing yellow light on Main Street and a tiny pitiful country store. There was a school that went from kindergarten through eighth grade. Then the students had to travel 20 miles to get to the high school. We had to go to the next town over to get to a decent grocery store, shopping center, pharmacy, hospital or even a doctor.

 Lord have mercy; don't let there be an emergency. By the time an ambulance got way out here the person was dead, buried and waving from the pearly gates. Nope! There was definitely not much out here. Just us poor folks trying to make it best we can.

Man if we wanted a day off from cooking, even that didn't come easy. Had to catch a ride and go all that way to town just to get a hamburger. It was sincerely rare that we didn't have to cook for ourselves. But I was willing to drive those long 20 miles every chance I got. Even the small town over was better than this hole in the wall.

To make things worse there was only a couple businesses that had limited supplies with minimal stock and exorbitant prices. Some might say and it was so, they had us by the tits and balls. We were forced to pay whatever they asked for the convenience of not traveling to the big stores that was definitely not down the street.

There was milk, bread, butter, cold cuts and jam. Flour, sugar, corn starch and ever baking need under the sun. Ripe fruits, vegetables and fresh butchered meats filled the old rickety cooler that was as loud as an old broken down truck with a cracked muffler. On the next shelf over there was pots, pans, cups, dishes, forks, spoons and utensils. In the same store there was paint, turpentine, camping supplies, potbelly stoves, shingles, plywood, bricks and cement. Whenever a customer would make a request the owner always ordered more than one and added it to the already over crowded store.

More than anything though, to the delight of every child around; was the sweets counter that was full of home baked cookies, cakes, tarts, puddings and custards. The candy ranged from soft caramels, hard sour balls, every delicious candy bar on the market as well as several homemade from the locals.

The store owner made sure that every girl and boy that entered the store did not leave until each one reached into the huge glass jar of multicolored gum balls and withdrew their favored color or flavor. When asked by the adults how much they owed, as they did each time; as though the answer might change on the present visit; the answer was always the same. The owner would look at the children, smile and wink as he proclaimed that the joy on those faces was the only payment he would take for those sweet little gum balls. He knew that he was dealing with a proud breed of people who did not want to accept charity as long as they were able to do otherwise. So saying that he was paid in smiles was satisfaction enough for everybody.

The corner store ran credit tabs for every family and each individual that they knew and trusted. The store owner kept little books in a rusty battered old can by the cash register. The workers rung up all of the stuff that was placed on the counter. As was known to happen and pretty often; when anyone ran short of cash, the shopper would just tell the cashier to put it on the books. Payday meant dropping some money by; without fail to make sure that the account stayed good. It was of the upmost importance to keep that tab in good shape. Times could and did get lean; real fast, quick and in a hurry. We had to be ready.

We all knew to leave doors wide open to make a way in times of trouble. If you were smart and I considered myself not to be the dullest spoon in the drawer, then you looked out for tomorrow. As people of lean days gone by and days that we knew were coming again; we always needed to be ready to make a way out of no way.

Those that did not prepare for the rough times, in times of plenty; paid steep prices when those terrible times arrived. Cause the bad times always came... again and again. The secret to getting through those times is to be ready. Ready we were. Ready we are. Ready we will be.

Chapter 17

Fake Fairytales

Just like the stores, men were few and far in between too. I was so very tired of looking and waiting. Tired of guys that wanted what was between my legs in the dark but didn't want to be seen with me in the light of day. All they wanted was those little bony stick girls. No sir, not a girl that had some meat on her bones.

Pretty and skinny couldn't cook or clean. Cute and thin couldn't keep a house or make something out of nothing. Bony and beautiful couldn't care for the kids, work in the fields and plan a budget all at once. Well let them have that itty bitty cutie pie; it would just be their loss cause those bones couldn't fill a belly or a heart.

You needed some real good meat to have them licking their fingers, their lips and to make them come back for seconds. I was the whole package and could do all of those things with one hand tied behind my back. I knew how to take care of business and of my man. I just needed someone to be my man.

If only someone would take the time to look behind all of this fluffy cuteness and see all of the good things that I am. Why didn't they take the time to see my heart? Inside of me is everything that they want to be in the skinny minis; but wasn't. All I know is the clock was ticking, ticking, ticking. I was desperately running out of prospects and time in this backwoods hick town.

Fairytales were not for people like me. No prince charming was racing in on his big white stallion to make my every dream come true. Heck, hadn't ever seen a prince in this lifetime and especially not around here. I know that I had run into a bunch of frogs and came across a few toads too. I'm not even mentioning all of the cockroaches, beetles, mosquitoes and fire ants. It is fake Fairytales for me...

I had the scars on my heart and mind; to prove that I had dealt with my share of losers. I was never going to acknowledge the wasted time and definitely wasn't letting on about the heartbreak, the rivers that are flooding the banks with my tears and the excruciating unending pain. All I could think over and over is, I was so tired of hunting for a fantasy that was never coming true.

I was praying and waiting for someone to love me... all of me. Waiting for someone to want me, inside and out. I kept looking. I kept hoping. I kept praying. I kept; even though I didn't want to, I kept waiting. I was so very tired. Tired of wanting. Tired of needing. Tired of waiting. Being tired and waiting was the constants in my life's story. At least I have a story. So I will just keep at it. I will wait.

I kept thinking that the world was lonely and ice cold. I just wanted something warm. A little heat might help everything. When I jumped into something, I jumped high. I jumped fast. That is how I ended up single with four little girls and no Daddies in sight.

I'm the girl that doesn't give up. I don't quit. I keep trying. That is why I was willing to jump again. This time though, I truly wished that I had sat my big butt down somewhere. But no not me. I jumped! I jumped high and fast; right into the fire.

What I didn't know was that the biggest, meanest, evilest devil ever was laughing his head off. He sat warming his hands in the fire that he had built just for me. And fool that I am, I jumped right in. Guess I should have kept waiting. Wished that I had been a little more patient. Then just maybe that crazy old devil might have passed me by.

Better the devil you know... at least that's what they said. Those old folk sayings were starting to drive me crazy about then. They were always popping up to remind me that I was making such a big mess by playing with fire. Except that I wasn't just playing with fire, I was playing with the devil himself. I just really would have preferred no devil at all. My life had enough going on without giving the devil full access to cause even more heartbreak, trouble, havoc and chaos.

All those wise old voices should have told me to skip the devil, step on the devil, slap the piss out of the devil, never kiss the devil and don't dare sleep with the devil. They should have told me to make sure that I kill the damn devil. Do anything, absolutely anything but fall in love with the devil! Guess they assumed that I understood the things not said, but obviously I didn't. By the time they started saying all that out loud and directly to me; I was in bed with the devil and he had me lock, stock and bond.

Hell, who listened to the old folks anyway? We figured that they just didn't understand us at all. We figured that they didn't know a love like this love. We figured that they had never been young and in love anyway. I guess I was fooled by all the sweet things that devil was shoving down my throat. The sad part is that I was swallowing every single drop up like it was water in the dessert. My tongue was hanging out of my mouth like a dog starving for a cool drink of some sweet sweet water. And I lapped it up every chance I got.

Chapter 18

Popping Gum & Spitting Lies!

I never figured it all out cause what I do know is that my hearing is as bad as my seeing. I refused to hear and I definitely didn't see it for what it was. I didn't listen when people told me that he was mean. I didn't listen to the men that said that he didn't like to work and couldn't keep a job. I didn't even pay attention to his relatives that said he had been troubled and messed up from birth.

I was ready to fight this girl that came up popping gum and spitting lies. She tried to tell me how evil he was. She told me that he used to beat her for breakfast, lunch and dinner. She said that he couldn't keep his hands off of her. She was going on and on. I tried to ignore her and walk off. She got in my way and refused to move. She kept spouting her stories of how controlling, horrible and cruel that he was.

I stood there until I had enough. I tried to mover around her but she would not move out of the way. She just kept going on about him being evil, a monster and the devil. I'd finally had it with all of that stuff. I told her to shut her lying mouth. When she didn't stop talking; I slapped the taste out of her mouth. I think she really got the picture cause she moved then. That heifer ran away faster than any gazelle that I had ever seen on the tv public broadcasting channel.

I didn't even listen to my own family that loved me and wanted good things for me. I walked away from many of them and it was disrespectful of me. But I couldn't let them stand in the way of my happiness. People changed, didn't they? I knew truckloads of things that they had done over the years. We loved them through it all. We forgave and forgot a whole lot of their mess. So why couldn't they give him a chance?

I didn't listen to my friends. If they kept talking bad about him then they became ex-friends real quick. They did not know him like I knew him. They did not understand that with me things would be different. They did not let people forget and move on. So they could get gone. Get out of my life and my happiness. I'm glad about my chance for happiness was finally here.

Chapter 19
Punching Bag

Everybody and their brother; all tried to warn me about the things that they heard about him. But I went off on them so crazily that it terrified the stuffing out of them. Shoot, I already know that most of them are scared of me and my crazy temper. So instead of pushing, pulling or fighting me about this stupid situation that I got myself into; they just shut up and left me on my own to figure it out the hard way. Guess the brick wall that they were warning me about was the one I would be bumping into real soon.

It was not easy that's for sure. I wanted to listen. The loneliness was covering my ears. I wanted to see. But the loneliness was a blindfold over my eyes too. I wanted what I wanted. Even if I had to go through hell fires to get it. Easy had never been the way of life for me. The hard way was the way for me cause I was not hearing any of it and that is all to it.

I wished and prayed that I had listened better to every single person around me. It was life shattering the first time he slapped me and I saw stars. Or the time when he punched me in the mouth and I had to each soup for weeks cause my teeth were loose. I will never forget the time when he hit me so hard in my stomach that it made me puke. I sadly think of the time that he shoved me off of the porch and my back was sore for a month. The time that he kicked me in the knee with steel toed work boots on; which amazed me cause he didn't work. I limped for months trying to get my knee back in order. The slaps, punches, pushes and beatings were too many to think of. I was his own personal punching bag.

I just wanted to forget it all. I wanted to continue wearing my rose colored glasses. I wanted to believe that I had love. Except that so many times of pain and hurt shattered my heart over and over again. Love should not hurt like this.

Of course, he apologized purposely. He was always so sorry for letting things get out of hand. He cried tears and begged me to forgive him. He always wanted us to move on and not stay in those bad moments. He did not want the bad times to last. I sure didn't either. But they kept happening, more and more. I wanted him to stop hurting me and to love me.

He told me terribly sad stories about his childhood. Told me how his father beat him with a horse whip until his back was strips of skin, gore and blood. Told me how his father had thrown the whiskey-still over and all of the hot liquid had burned his legs and feet. Then before the burns healed, his father had beaten him with a oak switch all over those burns. He told me that his mother had hit him in the head with a wooden stick until he passed out. The broom handle that had been used to beat him until it broke in little pieces was another of his pitiful recitals. He had been a beating ram for two crazy parents.

Every time that we had a bad time, then the childhood abuse stories would start again. The extension cord that had been taken from a broken tv set and used to whip him until he was senseless. The shovel that had hit him in the back after it had been heated in the trash fire was a whispered tale after a night of brutal pain. He told me about the long handled spoon that he had been sodomized with after his father had him drop his pants, hold on to his ankles and beat him with an oak stick until his butt was bleeding. Mercy God, who would treat a child like this?

That poor little boy had been through a whole lot. It was one terrible incident after another. But I could not understand why he would treat me like this after he had endured so much pain himself. He had to know the pain that he was inflicting because he had been through so much himself.

I was always an advocate for the wounded and the mistreated. I would never stand by and watch the underdog continue to be mistreated. I was willing to fight for the downtrodden. I could not stand by and let them get hurt. He told me that his mother never protected him from all of the beatings and pain that he had lived through as long as he could remember. I was trying to be there for him. I really was trying. But he made it hell; pure hell.

He was a childhood abuse victim that had become an adult brute. He was small and skinny so by beating on women, I guess that made him feel bigger. I wanted to forget all of this but I had lived it. So if I was being real and I am always real. This demon had become the devil himself.

He just wanted me to feel sorry for him so that I would let him stay. And I did let him stay all of those years cause I kept pitying him and putting myself aside. I couldn't stop thinking of that hurt little boy when he was crying like a baby after beating the snot out of me. I just wanted to hug him and give him the love that he had not gotten when he was a boy. I wanted the same love and support from him but all I got was pain and more pain.

I hid all of the scrapes, scratches and bruises. I covered up the pain, stiffness, hurt and dared not limp in front of people; especially not my family. Hell I could have been a professional makeup artist. I was a professional that should have been paid. It was a wonder; the way I slathered on that concealer and foundation. I was an award winning actress too. I could put on a show to cover up the pain, hurt and depression that would have amazed the best of them. I could act like nothing was wrong and nothing hurt; especially when I was near my babies. My name should have graced the front of many Oscars, Emmys and Globes cause I kept the performances top notch.

All of it was confusing deep down in my mind, body and soul. I couldn't wrap my mind around why I let this go on for so long. It was years of beatings, broken bones and sprains. My body had more scars, bumps and bruises than a prize fighter. Many days I looked like I had been in the ring with boxers like Muhammad Ali or George Foreman.

I got fed up every now and again. Then I would knock him on his butt just to get the pain to stop. I could have easily beaten the tar out of him. I could have mopped the floor with his skinny behind. I could have thrown him around like a frisbee. I just figured that he would leave and never come back if I didn't let him hit me, slap me, push and shove me or kick me. The last thing that I wanted was for him to go. Then I would be by myself again.

Chapter 20

Love Is Not This!

In my mind, those horrible painful times was the payment for those little bits of happiness. I wanted more than this. I deserved better. To my detriment, I just didn't ask or demand it. But my soul never stopped yearning for the bits of joy that my heart still needed but never got.

There were just so many long hard brutal years with only snatches of happy. To be honest, I don't know if it was any happy at all. I just lapped up and settled for whatever the devil bated me with to keep me in this hell on earth. It didn't make sense, even to me; especially to me. I just stayed anyway though. I just continued to wait. One day, hopefully, prayerfully, one day - my joy would come.

Love is not this and if anybody knew that; I did. I really did. I knew better, I swear I did. I just didn't do better. I knew it was bad, toxic, awful, horrible, cruel, violent, demonic and just plain retarded. But a few of those sweet moments would drive all of that crazy right out of my head.

People even told me that he might kill me but I couldn't see that. I wouldn't believe that. I refused to even think that. I just hugged my stuff tight, hung on for dear mercy and stayed. I refused to leave. I wanted to live. I wanted love.

I really truly did love life. I did not want to die. I was not staying in this waiting for that fool to go too far and kill me. I was not going to take this pain for too much longer. So I continued to wait for everything that devil promised. Even though I knew then. I know now. I will always know. The devil always was, he always will be and he absolutely, positively is a liar. That is so!

I kept looking the other way when he gave me those same tired old excuses. I listened to the warped repeated lies. I fell again and again for those scratched up, played out lines. I was trying to squeeze a little bit of happiness out of the crazy.

It seemed like a drop or two couldn't satisfy me. I acted like I was parched and thirsty. Every ounce made me desperate for my fantasy that I kept raising from the dead. That pitiful dream had been trounced and stomped on so many times that it was totally ridiculous.   If I saw it fading I would call a code and start CPR.

I would never stand by and just let my hope die. I held my breath and prayed like my life depended on it until the dream lifted it's weary head and blew it's breath out in a shaky sigh. I'd sniff it's death-like stale putrid scent and once again I would head to the waiting area.   Just knowing that my dream, my hope and my love was still alive only made me want more. It kept me thinking that maybe it just might blossom into every thing that I dreamed it to be; one day.

This was the only love that I had. Nobody else had ever taken a chance on me or stayed with me this long; before now. Even the men that I had babies with never took the time to listen to my hopes, dreams and desires. They did not even try to see my heart. None of the men in my past could see past the fat.   They never saw me. So I absolutely wasn't letting this man go. Without saying it out loud, I always thought "until you leave me" on his part. As for me it was always "until death do us part".

I was cherishing, treasuring and holding onto the tiny bits of happy that drizzled on me like the sweetest summer rain. I held tightest to the golden minutes when I felt like a girl dancing as the warm raindrops fell on my hot needy head. I clung to the times when the sweetness filled my mouth cause most times I felt like, no I knew; that I was utterly dying of dissatisfaction, disappointment, despair and despondency.

I referred to this state of mind to myself, as thirst. I was wilted, parched and needy. I remember when I was a girl and we would be out in the rain. The best part was sticking your tongue out to catch the sweet water in your mouth. Nothing was sweeter than those little bits of cool rain running down my throat. I was waiting for the sweet silken raindrops to just come again and satiate my never ending need as I held out my outstretched tongue.

I just wasn't watching the way those moments ran through my fingers like I had gaping holes in my hands. I didn't think of all of the wounds that had been soothed by those rancid waters. I was not thinking of the times times that blood filled my mouth choking me as it clotted in my throat. I didn't want to think of all of the bitter tears that ran down my busted cheeks and stung with their saltiness as they oozed onto my dry cracked split lips.

I was willing to endure the whispers as the sweat washed away my makeup and exposed the evidence of my pain. I lived with the devastating humiliation that I was bringing to myself, my Mama and my family by staying in this unhealthy place. I tried to lie to myself that nobody knew. Sadly, everybody did.

Even my babies knew. My girls were careful when they hugged me to avoid touching a sore place. Sadly they never kissed my cheeks cause I didn't want them to rub off my blush and expose the red on my cheeks from the slaps or fists that I had not ducked fast enough. I taught my babies early on how to help me hide my mistakes, my drama and my mess.

Who was I? What in the world? When did I become a wuss? Where was the strong woman that my Mama raised? Why was I letting this happen? Jesus Christ! What was going on with me? Why was I settling for bruises, broken bones, sprains and excruciating pain? Why was I teaching my girls and all of the young females around me that this is alright? This didn't just affect me. I can't believe I allowed all of this to happen to me, my life, my girls and my family.   Lord knows I have way too many questions and definitely not enough answers.

I had always taken care of me and everybody around me. I took great pride in myself.   I never stood by and watched a bad thing happen when I could do something about it.   Yet here I was with a ringside seat to the destruction of my body, my health, my mind, my pride, my love, my heart, my life but most importantly; my soul. Was I destroying others too? People that looked up to me, was I teaching them that this abuse was an acceptable way of life? It wasn't what I wanted to teach my girls or my little sisters. I knew better.   Lord, why wasn't I doing better?

I was a fighter not the beaten. I beat people up. I did not get beaten down. Not ever in my life before I encountered this devil. What had the devil turned me into? Better yet, what had I chosen to be for him; for love?   At least what was supposed to be love. This was definitely not it. That is for sure. I was the one that was big and bad. I was not the one whimpering waiting for the next fist or foot.

This thing had me dumbfounded.   I just could not understand for the life of me. Never ever let nobody even think of looking at me or mine sideways. I made excuse after excuse to myself about all of this foolishness. I lied straight to my own face.

So many days, I looked in the mirror and covered up cuts and bruises. I dared not look myself in the eyes. I would have died there and then. The shame and guilt would have choked the breath out of me. I just concentrated on every bump, scrape and blemish. Looking myself in the eyes might have revealed my sin sick soul. I have to admit that I just was ready to be done with all of this. I was ready to see all of me. It had been far too long since I had.

I would never have believed in a billion years that any man would have hit me. And I let him not only get away with it. But for some crazy reason, I let him live. It was sick that he could beat the crap out of me and I'd let him come right back. If it was anybody else, I'd just jump on 'em and beat the tar out of 'em. That's how it worked with everybody except for him.

I could not believe that I let things get like this. I let him shove me, slap me and kick me. I let him punch me and push me. I let him break my bones. I let him fracture several ribs. I let him hit me with a steel pipe and break my jaw. I let him gash my skull, get me 34 stitches and knock me out when he hit me over the head with my favorite crystal vase. So many injuries and I kept letting him come back. What was wrong with me?

I thought about all of this often. Sometimes it was all that I could think about. Lord help me understand how I could possibly let all of this crazy happen. There had to be a reason why I stayed in hell. It wasn't like the door was barred to keep me here. I wasn't locked in. I needed to lock the devil out. Instead, I was the fool over and over that let that evil back into my life.

Maybe I thought I deserved this hell. I could not figure any other reason. I had to be out of my ever-loving mind. Nobody should have to go through this, ever. But here I was going through this again and again. I was a fool because nobody; absolutely nobody deserved this unending torment. My ever day was purgatory on earth.

I could not blame anybody except me. I blamed me! I should have blamed him, but no. It was my fault for staying in this catastrophe. It was my fault for letting him get away with beating me day in and day out. I could have stopped him just by standing up for myself.

I probably could have popped his narrow behind in two. If I was being honest there was no probably to it. I could have clobbered this little wimp with my pinky finger. I let him do all of those things because I thought; no I believed... I believed that the excruciating bitter heartache, loneliness and pain of him leaving me would be way too much to bear. I believed I would die if he left. I just didn't want to believe that I would die if I stayed.

I chose to stay. I chose the pain. I chose the heartbreak. I chose the shame, degradation and depletion. The depletion of my pride, my self esteem, my honor and my get up and go. It had got up and gone a long time ago. It shamed me all the way from the top of my head to my tippy toes to let that little devil beat up on me. The guilt that I felt each time I looked into a mirror and saw me was unbearable. I did my best to stay away from mirrors, shining glass, stainless steel pots and even window pains. The very image of myself was never what I wanted to see and for sure it wasn't who I wanted to be. So I'd just keep imagining that the woman my Mama raised me to be was who I was going to become.

Chapter 21

<u>Forsake All Others!</u>

Truly, I couldn't stand the thought of him leaving me. Him leaving was a thought that I could not think. I didn't want to explain or answer questions to anybody but especially not to me. Because I had no explanations and no answers for none of us.

There is one thing that I know for sure and that is that I definitely didn't want to see him with somebody else either. I was his. He was mine. No piece of paper could make the vow more real. We were supposed to forsake all others until death do us part!

Living in this little town let me know the reality of the thought that continuously plagued me. I knew that if he wasn't with me I would be seeing him with whoever he ended up with. Everywhere I went I would be seeing him with a bony marony on his arm. That would tear my heart up way more than his fists ever did to my body.

I couldn't even think of being by myself again. I was just not ready to entertain the days and nights of no one in my bed or my arms. I was not standing by to be tortured even more than I already have been. No! Absolutely not! That was not happening. Love! Lord have mercy on my wayward soul. I just wanted to be loved. Everybody deserves some love in this life.

I realized that I had made a decision to be in this hell. Nothing was happening that I was not aware of. I had a sick obsession to accept whatever my torturer gave as long as he laced it with some affection, some kisses and some sweet lies. Yes. I decided to take the physical pain in my body cause I could not take the emotional pain in my mind or the heartbreak in my soul that was lurking at the mere mention of him leaving me and being with somebody else.

I remember one instance when my friends and neighbors came back from the club one night. I had stayed home cause my youngest daughter was sick. I told him it was alright if he went out but I warned him to keep his hands to himself. Told him to keep those girls' hands off of him too. It was a given for anybody that knew he was my man to keep their hands off of him; if they wanted to live that is. He didn't listen or they didn't listen. I don't know which.

All I know is that all those nosey gossips couldn't wait to run home and tell me that one of my young, skinny, pretty cousins was all over my man. They were talking all at the same time cause they wanted me to know all of it. They all had versions of her bony butt and how she was all in his face flirting hard and heavy. That dumb bald headed bimbo had made a great big deal of dancing in front of him and putting on a grand show. That hag must have been practicing to be a stripper or something. They said that she all but gave him a lap dance right there in front of everybody.

That foolish girl was young, cute, sexy, born skinny and dumb as a rock. She was obviously confused cause she must've thought that she was a showgirl in Vegas. Well this was as far away from Vegas as could be. She was going to find out exactly where she was. This was going to be a lesson that I guarantee that she would never ever forget as long as she lived.

This girl absolutely forgot who she was and where she was. And I know without a doubt that she definitely forgot who I was. I know that she had brain damage cause she knew better than to mess with me or my man. She must have a death wish or something. That heifer wore her clothes so tight, it looked like skin. That stupid girl was dumb with a little d. She thought that she was born to flirt with anything male. And I know that the garden tool never could resist the temptation of a penis. Well this was one that she should have skipped.

I thought about our family. It was clear that she didn't think about our family or about me. To her it was just another game. To me it was my life. Regardless of the fire that she was playing with, the fool forgot some things that she had been taught, I guess. Well I was willing to teach the dumbo a lesson or two. Starting with lesson number one: 'for every action there is consequences'. I was willing and able to deliver those consequences right upside her head. I was going to teach her the abc's of knowing better but not doing better.

That girl already knew not to mess with me. Hell! Everybody knew that I was nobody to play with. When I marked my territory, folks would rather walk through hell fires with gasoline drawers on than to play me. If I said it, I meant it and would be plenty happy to represent it.

So when I heard that she had the nerve to be up in my man 's face, I could not wait to see her. I went looking for the hussy. Checked her house, her friends and the community center. Thank her lucky stars; I couldn't find her no where. She sure should be plenty glad of that. Just made me know that somebody was praying hard for her.

My young cousin's luck ran out a few days later. The kids ran in saying that she was outside with my younger sister getting out of my neighbor's car. I saw red. For real, RED! My blood pressure must have gone through the roof. Time to pay the piper... Yes ma'am it was time to pay me for being up in my man's grill.

I called her in the house. She ran right in smiling and grinning like nothing was wrong. She probably thought that I didn't know about that night or about how she had acted. I told her to sit down. I was going to do the grown up thing and talk to her. I was only going to tell her to stay out of my man's face. I was going to give this garden tool in training a little bit of mercy.

But no! She showed me that it was not mercy time. It was kick ass time and worry about everything else later. See, I started talking to her. I was calm, cool and collected. I was telling her to learn how to act in public.

But this girl laughed.   She rolled her eyes and kept laughing. Then she got up and acted like she was going to walk up out of there. I waved her back to the chair. I was thinking to myself that my Mama would be proud because I was acting like an adult. But my cousin did not sit back down. Instead she was still laughing and not paying me any attention.

My young cousin had short hair. Real short hair that you could barely grab. I knew exactly how short it was because I had fixed her hair so many times over them years that I could not count. I had burned my fingers over and over with my straightening comb as I had tried to grab all of those little pieces of hair. I had tried to curl it. I had tried to braid it. I had tried to twist it up in cute little styles. I'd put hats on her head telling her that she was setting the style and everybody else was going to being wearing this style cause it was so chic. I lied most of the time. That bald head was not cute. But I did the best I could with it. Everybody and their brother had tried to help but nothing worked.   Home remedies and store bought bottles, tubes and jars of gunk.   Nothing worked. Everything that we tried to get that hair to grow was for nothing cause it stayed short, regardless.

I grabbed enough of it though to pulled her right up to my face. I let her look deep into my eyes. I let her see the rage that was boiling over like an erupting volcano. I let her smell the hot smokey smell of my breath so that she would know that the lava was coming. I held her up on her tippy toes to keep her off balance. I wanted her to know that she was trapped. I also wanted her to know that she was not going anywhere until I let her. Then she knew it was on.

Immediately she started screaming for her Mama. Well even if her Mama was here, it would not have saved her from this whipping that I was going to put on her bald head and narrow backside. She took turns calling for her Mama and mine. Honey chile neither one of them was here so come and face up. Guess she wasn't in the mood to laugh anymore. I was going to make sure that this lesson sunk in deep so that she would never forget this day. She was not going to mess with me or mine ever again.

I dragged her by those little pieces of hair like my baby girl drags around her rag doll. I pull her into the closest bedroom. All of the children in the house was screaming and crying. They knew that I was about to lose it. I know they thought that I was about to kill her. But no! I was not going to kill her. I was just going to make her wish she was dead. I guarantee that she was never going to play with me or my man again. Nope that'll never happen ever again. Bet cha bottom dollar on that!

I put her skinny bones on the floor between the twin beds in the boys' room. Got right on top of her and sat down. She could not move her skinny behind at all. All she could do was scream and holler. She was begging, pleading and promising with everything in her. It was not going to do her any good. She was getting exactly what she bargained for.

I grabbed the first thing that I saw. I got a high heeled shoe from under the bed. I don't remember hitting her. I know that I was wanting to hit her. I probably would have scared her and let her go, but she had started that laughing after I told her to sit down. That was her mistake. That laughing was playing in my head on repeat and that caused the room to go red again. Now I know it was probably nerves or just plain fear that had made her laugh in the first place. But that laugh was just more than I could take.

They said that I beat her in the head with the shoe until her head and face was a bloody mess. My oldest girl most likely saved her life. She had crawled up onto one of the twin beds. She was looking at me calmly and quietly saying the Our Father's prayer. That got my attention because it reminded me of my Mama and the way she said that prayer. I looked at my daughter with her head bowed, hands steepled, eyes closed, kneeling on that bed. It touched me and brought some calm into the room before I killed this girl. I stopped hitting her and threw the shoe down. When I let her up from the floor she was begging for mercy and promising she'd never go near him again. Yes sir! Now we in business. Better believe that she never did play with me or mine again. And that's the way it is supposed to be.

Sure that bit of crazy, caused some major family drama. Actually it caused a whole lot of family, friends, neighbors and everybody drama. Drama with a capital D. My Aunt wanted to call the police but we did not call them into our business back then unless it was life and death. That chick was living so that meant family would handle things.

Many folks thought I should be locked up. I know that they had always thought that I was crazy. Now they know that it's true. So not one of them were brave enough to come to say a word to me either. Guess they ain't crazy enough. Family was all talk; but not one of them crazy enough to approach me about that skinny chick, her bald head and her bloody face.

Mama got on me good. And she had the right to do just that. Even though I was grown, I was still her daughter. It made me so sad to disappoint, embarrass and hurt her this way. I hated when my crazy ran off onto her plate. I tried to take things off of her when I could. The last thing I wanted was to add baggage to her struggle. She had too much on her and I hated that I was shaming her this way. Lord knows that I didn't regret beating the stuffing out of my cousin but I did feel guilty about making Mama look and feel bad.

Yeah I get crazy but only when I am pushed to crazy. I know who I am. I really do. They better know too. And they better not forget it either. I know that they might have whispered behind my back but they made sure that they smiled in my face. Neighbors. Friends. Family. Scared of crazy, all of them. Hmmmm!

Chapter 22

Oak Trees Don't Move!

I was quick to put people in their place but I couldn't bring myself to get that demon straight that I slept with every single night. How many times had he hurt me? How many hospital visits and emergency room stops? How many bandages and homemade remedies to deal with all of the injuries that were not serious enough for a trip to the doctor? I knew the answer to every question... way too many and entirely too much.

The rabid dog had bitten me over and over again and again some more. I had been through so much for the little bit of so called love that I was getting back. It did not add up. The unrelenting pain and thousands of bruises was a steep price to pay for the tiny bit of love and affection I was getting. If it was love at all. It sure did not feel like I thought love should feel. How could all of this misery be worth it? It was not even close to being worth it at any point that I could possibly think of. If it was finally time to face reality, then I would have to admit that I did not know what love is at all.

I cannot count the amount of broken bones that I had had since he came into my life. He broke my collarbone, arm, leg, ankle, foot, thigh, back, fingers, my nose, jaw and some ribs over the years when his devil reared up. Mercy God I had so many breaks that I was absolutely sure that I would be full of arthritis way before I was fifty. At the rate he was going though, I might not make it to fifty. Hell at this rate I was not going to make it to forty. I was thirty-four. If I wanted to see thirty-five; some things had to change.

I could not count the amount of cuts, scrapes and bruises that he had inflicted on my poor body. I didn't even mention the sprains and fractures to add worse to wear. Sad but true, I'd had more injuries to this old body than people in battles and third world nations. I deserved a purple heart for the injuries that I had obtained in this bloody war that was my life.

I got extremely close to ending this love hate relationship many many times. One of those times was when we were driving on a country back road on a hot summer evening coming back from town. We had gone grocery shopping and was heading home to cook dinner. The Oldsmobile Delta 98 was clean and purring beautifully as it cruised along. I kept that car as shiny as new gold. It was gliding along so smooth and quiet that it could have been a boat on a calm sea. I had no idea that we were entering the storm of the century.

I was so entranced with the breeze blowing in my face and the smooth song that Smokey Robinson was belting out on the radio. I was looking at the oaks that stood along the sides of the road looking like bent and snarled old men watching over us as we floated on our way home. The leaves were heavy, bright green and so thick on the trees that the blue sky could only peek through here and there. The leaves were a canopy that provided a feeling of safety, comfort and calm. These times were the thoughts that you think of sweet summer days. It was a beautiful smoldering end of day that was settling down to let a tranquil peaceful evening take over; or so I thought.

It wasn't long before the calm was disturbed by his nasally whine. He was complaining about what the store was out of. We could not do anything about that so I kept concentrating on the beautiful day. Yeah! I was ignoring him cause he was going on about foolish things. At least it was foolishness to me.

I was trying to enjoy the beauty surrounding me and he was bleeding into my tranquility. I was concentrating on good things. I was keeping my mind positive hoping it would bleed out into the car. He kept growling meanness about the people at the grocery store. Who gets evil about groceries?

There are things that you can control and that was not one of them. I just wanted to enjoy the sunny day and the great dinner that I was going to cook. He was doing everything that he could trying to spoil this beautiful summer evening. The mess he was trying to bait me with was not worth fighting and losing out on the beauty all around us. I was not answering back the way he wanted me to. I kept looking out the window thinking about the delicious meal that I was going to cook when I got home.

I should have listened better cause he started yelling about teaching me so that I would learn to listen. As I turned from the window I saw the crazy in his eyes but it was already too late. Too late to listen or to learn. Too late to get this train back on the track. Too late to put the plug back in the bottle. Too late to right the ship that was teetering in the storm. It was too late Lord.

That's when the crazy erupted like a volcano. The fire burned me immediately. The fool reached over while I was still looking out of the window and he pushed my head into the dashboard. It was so fast that I did not know what hit me. I saw stars and blackness as I heard a loud screeching scream. Then I realized that it was me screaming.

Just when I told myself to stop screaming and my vision started to clear just a little; I saw that giant oak coming right at us and fast. Why was it getting closer when we were supposed to be driving on the road; not towards the trees. It was then that I knew that he was trying to kill me. That mean, evil, cruel old devil did the absolute unthinkable. I started screaming again and he drove my side of the car right into a huge old oak tree.

When I came to, apparently I had passed out either before or when we hit that ginormous oak tree. He was crying and hollering louder than me while we waited for the ambulance. I was entrapped by the dash that had me pinned so that I could barely move. I could not have gotten out if I wanted to.

I was terribly hurt, bleeding, moaning and crying out to God not to mention hollering now and then for my Mama. I was in and out of blackness. Every time I came to, I looked at him to see where he was hurt cause he was hollering so much and so loud. One time I woke cause he was slapping me. Slapping the taste outta my mouth like the old folks used to say. He was slapping me so hard that I was choking on the blood in my mouth. Why was this fool slapping me, hollering my name and hurting me more when I was already in more misery than I could possible imagine.

I told myself that I absolutely had to stay awake. I spit a big wad of blood at him that I was coughing and gagging on when I came too. No sir! I was not going to drown on my own blood. This demon was on a mission to destroy me. I had to stay awake even though sweet soothing sleep would have taken me away from all this pain. I knew that it was dangerous to sleep when you were hurt. There was no way I was going to sleep myself to death. No I was staying awake pain and all.

I was clinching my teeth so hard bearing the pain that I was sure I was going to break my teeth. I was hurting so bad. He was screaming his head off so he must be in terrible pain too. He might need my help so I was fighting that sweet darkness that was trying to woo me away from this excruciating, burning, screeching blur of pain that was my body. I tried to ask him where he was hurt but I could not get it out; between the pain and trying not to choke to death on my own blood.

I did everything that I could to focus. I prayed. I thought of my girls. I wanted to see them and raise them. Lord knows I wanted to see my Mama again. I had to hang on. I wanted to live. I had to live for my babies. They needed me. My family needed me.

Mama needed me too. We were a team that was raising my girls and her younger ones. They were not all grown yet. I had to help raise all of those churn. Taking care of home, cooking, cleaning and raising churn was always a part of my gifting. It is what I did best. So I had to keep doing it. I could not leave yet! I had to live. To live, I had to stay awake.

I quieted myself and concentrated hard on not fainting. I heard piercing loud screams. Wait a minute, now. I closed my eyes and listened hard. What was going on? I was not screaming. The screams were not coming from me. I was sure of that. So where were they coming from?

I turned my head towards him and almost passed out from the pain. Everything around me turned white, red, foggy and blurred out. I swallowed hard and forced myself to stay away. It was him. Oh my God! It was him. Jesus! It was him. He was the screamer. The devil was screaming like no tomorrow. Loud, high pitched, ear piercing, whining screams. Screams like a little girl crying for her Mama.

I almost started laughing thinking he sounded like my girls when they skinned a knee or fell and hurt themselves. But merely trying to smile was too much. I almost threw up from the wave of pain that assaulted me. I needed to listen to him so that I could figure out how bad he was hurt. I would do what I could to help him.

This had to be an accident. Right? An animal must have ran out into the road and cause us to swerve trying to miss it. A car must have ran us off of the road and left before I came to. Man! I had not seen an animal or another car. But there had to be an explanation. This was not real.

What had happened? I kept saying over and over that this just had to be an accident. No... there was no animals. No... there was no other car. It was time to face the facts. He had tried to kill me. I could not believe this. He drove into a tree. I did not want to believe this. He drove off of the road and hit a tree on my side of the car. He did this on purpose. He was evil. Evil to the bone. Evil through and through.

This screaming crying demon was begging me to understand that I had made him totally crazy. He thought he was going to lose me. He was begging me not to die. He was slapping my face and trying to wake me up. He was telling me that this was all my fault. What the hell was this fool talking about?

He actually said that none of this would have happened if I had just listened to him. He kept telling me all of the things that I had done to make this happen. I was stunned. Stunned, flabbergasted and in severe pain. What did he mean? I wasn't driving, he was. So how did I do this? How did I make this happen? My fault? How in the world was this my fault? It could not be. It was not my fault. All I remember was sitting quiet, enjoying the ride, taking in the scenery and planning a mouthwatering unforgettable meal in my head.

I spit a mouth full of blood and a few teeth out. At least I wasn't choking and gagging as much now. I took a deep breath and then several more. It make things a little clearer. Yes. Just breathe and it will be alright. I painfully and with great effort, turned to him. Then I almost fainted. Not from pain or the injuries. Pure unadulterated rage ran through my veins like blood. My fault? My fault? I caused this? How? Why? What the hell?

I swallowed the hot vomit back down that rose in my throat every time I moved. I tried to focus but my eyes had salty sweat or blood in them and it was hard to see. But when I finally got them open and I could see him; I almost fainted from the shock of it all. Lord have mercy on my soul and on his soul too. Cause if I got any part of my body to move then he might be seeing God in person today!

He looked as clean and put together as when we had left home. There was sweat running down his face but his shirt didn't have a wrinkle on it and the crease on his pants leg could have cut like a knife. He was sitting under the steering wheel and leaning towards me. I forced myself to open my eyes and then I saw this for what it was. He didn't have a single cut, bump or bruise anywhere. Yet he was screaming like a banshee. We had hit an oak tree. No. Me and my beautiful car had hit an oak tree. He had driven me into the tree. As usual, after one of his fits; I was the only person that was left hurt.

The devil himself had tried to kill me. He had tried to steal my life. I was playing with fire. All I know is, if I didn't stop warming my hands here and now; this fire was going to burn me all up. I should have been strong enough to walk right on out of his life then and there. Hell I should have been running as fast as my broken bones could take me with those hell hounds on my tail. But the pain I felt let me know that I would not be running or walking anywhere for a very long time.

He cried all over me begging and pleading before the police and ambulance came. He told me what to say to save him. All that begging, tears and pleading must have gotten through my river of blood and the crazy pit of pain that I was drowning in. Some of those tears and pitiful words, pierced my beat up heart. Pain or not, I already knew that I wasn't going anywhere. I was crazy in love or just plain crazy. Whatever it was, oak tree or not; I was staying, again.

I was in the hospital for a very long while recovering. I did not tell the truth about the incident because it was not an accident. I told my Mama the truth. I saw the hurt and disappointment as she looked at me with tears running down her face. I could see the questions in her eyes but she did not allow them to pass her lips. I know that the guilt and shame was oozing from every pour that I owned.

I had promised her that nothing else was going to happen when I went back last time. Here I was right in the middle of the craziest mess that I could not even think of. I deserved the shame and guilt. She knew it. I knew it. I had chosen to stay in this hell with crazy demon-boy. But my Mama would never add to my pain. That is not who she was. She did not put me in a position to shame myself even more than I already was. She let me keep what little bit of dignity I had. Trust and believe, I did not have much. Probably only a tiny itty bitty speck left after all of this.

Then I almost lost my mind. I saw a sleeve near my door in the hallway. I recognized that shirt. Jesus! No! Please no! But God was not going to answer this prayer today. I knew exactly who was standing at the door listening. Just knowing that she had heard every word took that speck of dignity and slapped me right up side my head with it.

It made me crazy to see my oldest girl peeking around the door when I called out to her. Oh Lord! I had no clue that Mama had brought her to the hospital. Most kids would not want to come anywhere near needles, sickness and medicine. But my oldest was curious about everything. She wanted to learn about everything and took every chance that she got to learn more.

Lord have mercy on my sick soul. That meant that Mama knew the truth and now this young girl did too. The last bit of dignity leaked right out of my soul through my swollen eyeballs as it mixed with my bitter tears that stung every single cut on my busted up face as my daughter stood looking at me.

Oh God! I was destroying my body, my own self esteem and now I was damaging my own daughters with my actions and my example. I was truly ruining them too. That is the very last thing in the world that I ever wanted to do. This was wrong. Letting them know that I chose to stay in an abusive relationship was so bad. I needed to do something to save them but most of all; to save myself.

This was totally not okay. I was teaching them to let men treat you any kind of way. I was showing them that they should stay in a mess when the man did not honor them, treat them well or even love them. I was saying that it was alright to be beaten, battered and abused; then stay for more. I was telling them to think of what they wanted first and their babies later. Oh God!

I needed to change some things in my life so that I could save the lives of the little girls that God had given me. My younger sisters, female friends and family members not to mention my little girls were watching me and learning from me. God help me, I have no clue how many lives I am affecting by going through all and by staying in all of this.

I know that I was being selfish in a crazy way but... Wait! No more buts. I was being a horrible example to all of the women in my life and especially to my daughters. I know if anyone treated them like this evil demon had treated me for years; I would be in jail. No! I would be in prison because I would kill the man that put their hands on my girl churn. I would choke the life out of that male dog with my bare hands. I definitely would not let them live.

But here I was letting this crazy fool get away with treating me worst than anything that I have ever dreamed. The hypocrisy of it all was more laughs than the comedy zone on tv. I was laughing my head off suddenly. Mama just quirked her eyebrows at me in a questioning way. I muttered in between laughing, "One thing that I will never forget is that Oak trees don't move!"

She started laughing with me. I was laughing through my tears but I knew I was having a moment. My Mama just nodded her head. I think, no I know that she understood that I had a life changing revelation right then and there.

I could not teach my babies, my sisters and all of the young women in my life, all of these bad things. God help me but I could do bad without adding more bad on top of it. The oak tree won't move but I sure can!

Chapter 23

<u>Rabid Dog In My House!</u>

Before I could tell my Mama about my revelations, the doctors came into my room. They had tons of questions about the "accident". They were firing them at me like shotgun pellets. Every face in the room was looking at me. The vomit burned the back of my throat as I looked from face to face. Sweat was running down my back like a raging river. I thought I was going to faint several times.

I realized immediately that I could not tell them the truth. I couldn't. God knows that a big part of me wanted to tell it all right then and there. But that is not what I decided to do. I told them that a dog or a deer or some animal; I am not sure which, had run into the road. I told them that he was trying not to hit the animal, lost control of the car and then, we hit the tree.

I looked down the whole time. I spoke quietly and I am sure that they were all straining to hear me. My waving squeaky voice was barely louder than a whisper. They probably thought my throat was hurting but my heart was hurting so bad that I thought I was going to die of a heart attack. I just couldn't face any of their knowing eyes. Those eyes that suspected and most likely knew that I was lying. If I had looked up and saw pity; it would have broken me. I looked at my folded clenched hands that were trying not to tremble like his life depended on it. Because it did.

The head doctor gently touched my hand and told me to get some rest. As they all followed him from the room, I almost smiled. They looked like baby ducks following the Mama duck. Mercy, how could I find humor in the middle of all that lying? After the last one left and closed the door, I closed my eyes and took a long soothing cleansing deep breath. I needed something to clean all of that muck right out of me. I tried to stop shaking while I was telling myself over and over that I had done the right thing.

When I opened my eyes and looked around the room; it was then that I saw my oldest girl sitting in the chair across the room. She had been so quiet that I had forgotten that she was here.

We would have sent her out when all of those doctors came but she had not made a peep and we forgot that she was curled up in the chair in the corner reading a book that she had gotten from the library.

Oh Lord! Here I go again making a mess into a even bigger mess. That Rabid Dog lived in my house and I let him! That dog had bitten me so many times that I had lost count. Now with those old soul eyes staring at me; I felt like he bit me again right then and there.

My daughter was looking directly at me. Those hazel eyes were bright green and full of tears that had not fallen. Her eyes were trained on me and she was not going to look away until I dealt with her. I went back to shaking like a leaf on a tree in a bad windstorm.

Those tears were breaking my heart and they had not even left her eyes. This girl rarely cried. She had gotten spankings and refused to shed a tear. People had died in our family and while she looked sad, she had not cried at any of the funerals. Those tears were rare and extremely precious. But today watching her Mom lie to all of those doctors had her eyes full of tears, her skin paler than I had ever seen it and her cheeks red as maraschino cherries.

My Mama knew that I was about to freak out. I was going to lose my ever-loving mind. I was not sure what to do. I was frozen like an ice cube. Mama came closer to the bed and handed me the water bottle that was on the bedside table. I looked at her in my complete desperation. Mama closed my hands around the water bottle and told me to drink all of it. I took my time drinking that water and looking at my hand that was clenching the bed spread.

Eventually I knew that I had to face my first born baby who was now a young lady. That smiling girl that was always happy and cheerful; had the saddest look that I had ever seen on her face since she was born. Jesus Christ! I put that sadness in her. I did that. Here I was showing her how to protect a bad person in his evilness. I was teaching her to lie. I was showing her how to let somebody hurt you and get away with it. How could I do this? Lord knows I felt like I had no choice.

I would get rid of him. I would. Soon too. I just wasn't letting the jails get him. I know how many terrible things could happen if he was in jail. I did not need that guilt too. That is exactly what I told my oldest when those doctors left the room.

I explained to her that I had enough on me wondering if I was going to walk right again with a broken leg and if my arm was going to heal right after two surgeries and possibly more to come. I made her smile a little when I told her that I had enough plates in me to have a rich lady's China sale. I got a bit of a giggle when I told her I had so many bolts and screws that I could open a hardware store. I would rather have her laughing then crying any day.

Jesus what was I doing? Mercy God! My oldest daughter was already dating. Sometimes she brought her boyfriend over to my house. They were good kids just trying to figure themselves, the world and love out. They were in the middle of their first love. It was so sweet to watch them together.

I hoped and prayed that she could keep that kind of love all of her life. The kind of love that I wanted but never had. The kind that was sweet, true and real. The kind that was patient, kind and lasts. The kind that is not rude, not proud, not boastful, not envious, not selfish, not easily angered, not holding wrong doing and not evil. The kind that celebrates truth, protects, trusts, hopes and is forever. The kind that never fails.

They spent a lot of time with me. I would cook for them and let them hang out in the music room. I kept all the latest albums, eight track tapes and tape cassettes. I had a stereo, a tv set and a couple comfortable sofas in there. I had big pillows on the floor and it was a totally cool place to hang. They did not have money so this was a fun and cheap place for young love.

I know that they listened to me and I tried to tell them so much so they wouldn't fall into the traps that I had. I tried to teach them to be safe and to enjoy themselves. I thought that I had done right by her. But here I was teaching her that it was alright to let a man hurt you, then stay and now lie to protect the very one that hurt you. Oh Lord! God was going to get me for this. I knew this could not end well if I did not end this craziness.

It was cemented right then and there when she walked over to the bed, looked me in the eyes and told me that she would not tell anybody about what really happened with the oak tree. I cringed and started shaking my head no. I could not get a word out. All I could do was shake my head.

My Mama touched her shoulder and she turned and walked out of the door into the hallway. Mama stroked my hand and said a short prayer. It calmed me as it always did to hear her pray. She told me to rest and let me know that she would be back soon. She told me that we would talk then. But there was one thing that she wanted me to thing over, "Rabid dogs don't get well. They are sick. They stay sick. And they will bite you again and again."

Chapter 24

The Eye Of My Storm

All I know is I was not letting him go to jail. I just couldn't. I would have been worried silly about that man. He was a black man. Them white jokers were hard on black men in jail. Some came back broken and changed forever. Some left their manhood and their minds behind those bars.

Most times we definitely didn't get back what we put in. Some of our men only came back to us in pine boxes. Oak was craved by every housewife but that's one box that I did not need. I did not care how bad every single part of my body was screeching in pain; they were not getting another black man up in that jail because of me. Nope not today.

Mama and my oldest left the hospital and went home to look after the other children. I felt terrible that she had to work, take care of everybody, cook, clean and do all the things that I was used to doing. But I couldn't do a thing. I was here laid up in a hospital because that monster had driven me straight into an oak tree.

The realization of it all was mind blowing. I was in wonder thinking about the last few days when a black light skinned lady with a long ponytail walked by my open hospital door. I saw her hesitate and peek inside. Then she started walking off. I thought that was good because I was really wiped out after the visit with my Mama and my oldest girl. It had been traumatic for them but it was still killing me.

Then I saw that lady turn around, walk back by and hesitate again. She was looking in here like she wanted me to ask her to come in. She was at the wrong room. Cause I didn't know her. She didn't know me. So I wasn't asking her anything. She may as well go on her merry way cause she was not wanted up in here.

But the lady was not going anywhere. She was standing by the door humming. Why was she humming here? I decided to close my eyes and pretend that I was sleeping. I did not want another visitor right now. I lay still and quieted my breathing because I felt her looking at me from the doorway. Then she started humming louder.

She was humming one of Mama's favorite old gospel songs: "Trouble in my way. I have to cry sometimes. So much trouble. I lay awake at night. But that's alright. I know my Jesus, He will fix it - after while."

I kept my eyes closed and she kept humming. Finally I figured I may as well open my eyes cause this lady was not leaving. What was wrong with her? Geez! She sure could not take a hint. Besides, I wanted to know why she was at my door and why was she staring at me. That lady did not know me. So why was she looking at me like I was a piece of art on display in a museum. Hell I am in here hurting. Anybody with eyes could see that.

When my eyes fluttered open again, I saw that she was standing in the edge of my room leaning against the door jam. She had a peaceful dreamy look on her face that was uplifted to the ceiling. Alright now I understood it. She was a Bible thumper or one of those witness people that bothered everybody like a fly buzzing in your ears a face.

This lady was already irritating and she had not said a single word. She stood in the doorway leaning with her eyes closed and a small smile on her lips. She acted like she was exactly where she wanted to be. Which I certainly did not understand. Well guess it was time to face the music.   Cause she was rocking a little and humming like her very life depended on it.

Then she opened her eyes and we were staring at one another.   She stopped humming and stood there for a minute. She asked if I was alright. I asked her if I looked alright.   She smiled and said that I looked pretty good considering what I had been through. I wondered if she had any clue what I had been through. She did not know me and she definitely did not know my business. Besides that she could go on somewhere else and put her nose in somebody else's beeswax.

She asked if it was alright if she prayed for me. I cut my eyes at her and mumbled that I had no clue why she was asking cause I already know that she was going to pray anyway. So she may as well get it over with and leave so I could get some sleep. That made her laugh and it settled some of the tension in the room. I wanted to smile a little when she started laughing that way.

She walked over closer and sang a little of the song that I was so familiar with. It was normal to hear Mama sing bits and pieces of it when she worked around the house or while she sat in her favorite recliner by the window and hand sewed her quilts. As she got to the end of the song, she started humming again.

I laughed inside so as not to hurt her feelings. Always could tell them Baptist Church Ladies. They did not know how to end a song without getting a round of humming in. A little bit of a giggle almost came out but smiling with my tore up lips stopped that in it's tracks. Then she laid her hand gently on me. She prayed her heart out and started humming again. I had to admit that I did feel a sense of calm, quiet and peace come over me while she prayed. Just maybe it wasn't that funny after all.

I thought she would leave then. But, no. She stood there quietly looking at me like she was waiting for something. She said that if I needed to talk I could. I let her know that I had plenty of people to talk to. She nodded her head and placed a pamphlet in my hand. I looked at it and started to crumble it up in her face. But I could not do that. I had better manners than that. Besides I was not bringing anymore shame on my Mama. I had already done enough of that.

I put it on the tray in front of me. She picked it back up and put it in my hands. She looked me dead in the eyes and told me in a very stern voice to read it. Then she cocked her head to the side like she knew something that I didn't. She nodded her head like she was answering a question with a slight quirk on her face. I don't know what questions she was answering because I had not asked anything.

I stared back at her like we were in a staring contest like the kids did. The first one to look away would lose. I was not losing today. I had already lost enough. She nodded again and gave me her biggest smile. I didn't know what to do so I looked away. Seemed like she cheated to win our little game to me.

She laughed a little and patted my hand. Then she said that she would continue to pray for me. She would pray that I would know that I was loved and most importantly that I would leave and live. I looked at her like she had lost her mind.

She told me that she was here praying because she had made that very choice. "What choice?" I whispered. "Leave and Live." she said. I just stared at her. "Child the storm will come again . Nobody wants to be caught out in the middle of the storm. The storm will come again and again. Get inside and away from the danger. Girl being uncovered in the middle of the storm can kill you. You can die if you stay. You got too much to live for. Them little girls need you bad for that. I hope you hear me girl."

She patted me and started humming again. She turned around at the door and looked at me hard. She whispered, "He is a sick, abused, mental little boy. Ain't nothing you can do to heal him. You ain't no doctor. You can not make him well. He ain't no better than a rabid dog. Leave and live girl!"

She looked me in the eyes the whole time that she talked to me. Then she quirked her head to the side again and acted like she was listening to that something that onLy she could hear. She nodded her head yes, stood straight up and straightened her shirt. She smiled a tiny smile and placed her hand over her heart as she looked deep into my eyes. The humming started up as she left the room and headed down the hospital hallway. I strained to hear that humming until I couldn't hear it at all. I just imagined that I did for a long while as I sat there.

I thought about throwing the pamphlet into the trashcan that was sitting near my hospital bed. But I could not do that. It had to be a reason that this lady singing Mama's song had come to pray for me. She acted like she knew my story or something. She acted like she knew me. She had come to pray for me... She could have visited others but she had come to me. Obviously God was trying to tell me something. So I turned the pamphlet over, opened it and closed it again. I went over what she said in my mind. I took a deep breath as I opened the pamphlet for the second time. I decided that I would like to; no I needed to read her words.

The Eye Of My Storms

My Test Became My Testimony

The eye of the storm can be the calmest part at the center of the storm. It was always the most intense part of my tumultuous situation. On land the center of the eye is, by far, the calmest part of the storm, with blue skies and soft rains while the outside bands are raging and crazy. Those outside bands, however it's the most dangerous. The water is raging as ocean waves from all directions are crashing and eroding the shores. The storms create enormous size waves that wreak havoc on my surroundings. It's the small zone of calm in the midst of chaos that is ferocious and batters everything in it's path with such devastating destruction as it kept trying to destroy my life.

The enormous walls of wind and rain that swirl around this quiet respite of the eye are the exact polar opposite of the storm bands. Those winds lash out with the cyclone's greatest and longest lasting fury. Unstable air turbulence, low pressures and rising unstable motion is the ultimate key to building the perfect storm. Sadly it's true; I have known far too many storms.

There were times when my life was at its best. Everything seemed to be going really well. The relationship was at its strongest peak and we tended to be working as a team. Everyone seemed to be having fun or so you want to think. These are the times when the warning signs are at their greatest. Nothing is what it seems though. It's actually the calm before the rage. It's the time right before all hell breaks loose. It's a temporary lull in what's going on inside before it explodes to the outside. There is a surety that within, that life as it has been is about to change forever. There will be no going back once the explosion occurs. The damage will be life changing and devastating.

Growing up in church with my Dad as the Pastor as I was being groomed to eventually take over his church was always my focus and my heartfelt prayer. I was born to follow in his footsteps. My Dad did many things in the community, especially with young people. So I was busy helping bring his vision to past. I taught Sunday school, instructed the weekly bible class, while also serving as a choir director. There is no wonder that I chose Teaching as my profession because I was teaching as long as I can remember.

One weekend the Church was having a community skating event. We loaded up several buses of young people. I was home from college to help my Dad with this event. As I was counting young people that boarded the bus; in walked a tall, beautiful caramel brown skinned young man. He was smart, sophisticated and sexy. It was so evident with his charm, swagger and the striking letterman's jacket that he wore from a well-known all-male prep school. That all meant money, handsome and smart all rolled up into one. Just what all of us girls were looking for in a guy. The best thing of all was that he was looking at me.

We connected immediately and dated for many years. He was caring, attentive and just an all-around fun guy. He would come and visit me while I was away in college. Our relationship began to grow. We were as tight as two peas in a pod. We were inseparable. We did everything together. Eventually we went to the next level, which led to marriage and children.

For the first few years everything was going well. There were small signs, but I thought I could pray them away. It seemed like the more I prayed, the worst things got. One day we were at his Mom's house and he got very angry. I decided I was going to take the kids and leave. He was not having that. He double bolted the locks and took the key out of the door to prevent us from leaving. He essentially held us hostage with his rage.

I was holding the kids, crying and praying. He was enraged as he screamed for me to stop praying. His mom was begging me to stop praying too. But I knew, with everything in me; if I stopped, I would die. See he had choked me to death one day, long before we got married. I saw bright beautiful lights and the heavenly gates. The Lord told me to go back. I did. Eventually I came to, disoriented on the floor with no place to go. These were signs that I refused to see. I thought I could fix this. The young man that I loved had just lost his father, so I gave him a pass. I credited his grief instead of seeing the situation for what it was. He later told me that I was convulsing and that he thought I was dead. I didn't realize all this had happened to me, until many years later, when he told me that he thought that he had killed me during the incident. It was so scary to hear. The neighbors heard me screaming and they called the police. I did not remember any of it. This was day that was the beginning of my storm. The clouds were forming, swirling and getting darker by the second.

Very, very quickly he got his hooks into my heart and my life. And just as quickly it turned from absolutely amazing whirlwind romance into the storm of the century. The cracks started to appear as he became emotionally abusive and extremely critical. Then the storm started to rage even greater as physical abuse became a regular occurrence in our marriage. Each time, he profusely promised that he would never do it again. The winds would quiet and the rain would cease.

Then suddenly with little or no warning, the storm would start to rage all over again. It got easier and easier for him to put his hands on me. The violence would escalate quickly. One night he kept hitting me and our son who was 7 years old, walked in on it. My husband sent him to his room. Our son would not leave. He just kept standing there looking at him hit me. My husband, our son's Father; preceded to tell our little boy that this is what to do when Mommy is not obedient, as he placed a pillow over my face. I look back on this and realize that my son being there, probably saved my life that night.

There were low and high pressure that built up before the storms erupted. Now some might think that my husband was on drugs or was drinking when he was abusive. But no he was completely sober. He could not use alcohol or drugs as an excuse. He was supposed to be in control of his own faculties but I did not think mentally that this was a fact. He apologized with every excuse under the sun including grief, stress and the pressures of life. There was no excuse that could support the verbal, emotional, physical and sexual violence that he inflicted on me.

My storm was raging out of control at this point. My Mother-in-law told me later that he was abused by his own Father. He was the son of an abuser. The abused became the abuser. Some might have stopped praying. But, no! Prayer kept me. My faith sustained me. God was with me.

I constantly prayed that my husband would stop, repent, change and fix our marriage. We had a family with small children to raise. We could have overcome the statistics that were forecasting the demise of our family. Instead the violence continued to swirl all around us. I would leave for a while to let things calm. Then he would come get me with promises that he loved me and he would never hurt me again. I'd think the that just maybe the storms were over.

I was looking for a rainbow. A covenant vow that the storm was over. I tried to believe, hope and pray. Until the next time I heard the thunder. I wanted it to be different. And they would be for a little while. But low and rumbling thunder continued to echo in the background to remind me that the storms were coming. Things would sometimes be great for a while. This man was a charismatic charmer. Everyone who met him thought he was a great guy. He was friendly and met no strangers.

No one knew like I did; the rage that lived inside of him that rained from his fists like lightning bolts as they struck my body. The eye of the storm, even in the midst of great times did not give me peace. I knew that the storms were still out there. I knew that it was on a matter of time until they came again. As the thunder rumbled, our great times were getting shorter and shorter.

It has been said that leaving an abuser is rarely a one-time event. The statistics say that successfully exiting an abusive relationship can take an average of seven times. Tornadoes came through our lives because each time I returned to him, the period of calm got shorter and shorter. I was constantly waiting for the quiet before the storm to end.

I thought it was a classic scenario. We were in love. Our pheromones were as crazy as a dust storm. We were whirling and twirling as we strolled in the summer rains not realizing that it could turn into a thunderstorm at the drop of a hat.

This man was very, very charming. The molecules would change in the air when he walked into a room and people would gravitate towards him. He had a powerful personality that was incredible and everyone was fooled. He was electric, magnetic and so dynamic that one minute, we were on top of the world then in the next the rage would become a tsunami. There'd be a flash of temper and then he'd become very critical of me. Then suddenly; he would be physically enraged.

One day, while we were separated; my husband came by the house. I opened the door and it appeared that it was a beautiful sunny day. I was getting our kids ready to go to a church picnic. He wanted to take our kids to his family reunion. He had not notified me about the event. I told him that we already had plans. The air crackled with electricity of the coming storm.

The argument began as he pushed me. I sent the older children downstairs. There was a young couple renting my basement apartment. I picked our crying baby up hoping to calm the storm. Even with our baby in my arms, that did not stop him from pushing me around. The husband of the girl down stairs came up to keep him from hurting me. The girl took the baby from my arms, so that our baby wouldn't get hurt. He pushed me against the kitchen sink hard and threw a glass at me.

My own storm started to swirl. I grabbed the butcher knife off of the sink and took off after him. The tenant grabbed me and placed me on the stairs to keep me from hurting my husband. I was crying and praying at the top of my lungs. He was at the bottom of the stairs mocking me and God. He accused me of talking to the devil. I told him that my God was with me. The proof of that lied in fact that he was still alive. The police was called. He left when he heard them coming.

Circling just outside the of the eye of a hurricane are winds that make up the eyewall. They're the scariest, nastiest, loudest part of the storm. The storm kept escalating until I realized that eventually one or both of us were going to die if the storms did not cease. He constantly watched and followed me. I was going to chair rehearsal on night. I knew that he was following me. The thunder was getting louder. The wind was rising. I had a van full of church kids. Thunder boomed. My husband came out of nowhere and blocked me. Lightning flashed. He jumped out of his car and slashed my tires. The kids were terrified. He drove away while I tried to calm the church kids. The storm receded as quickly as it began.

That was not the final straw. No! Another storm had to make me realize that it was far too dangerous not to come in out of the life threatening weather. One night we were in bed. The baby would not go to sleep. She was restless, crying and fighting sleep. He got so enraged that he threw the remote control and it hit me in the mouth. Abuse rained down on me like a hailstorm with golf ball sized hail. I tried to leave with our kids. He would not allow it. He took my wallet, keys and money. He shoved me out into the street during a winter blizzard in just my underwear.

I walked in the night to my sister's with only cold wet snowflakes swirling around me to cover my nakedness. They wrapped me in a blanket and called the police. My injuries were significant. My busted lip needed sixteen stitches not to mention the healing that the rest of my body, my mind and my soul required. My husband was sent to jail. I packed my children and as much possessions as I could into my car.

My family had recently moved South to find better weather. I was finally ready to feel the sun on my face and the warm winds to sooth my battered body, my trodden down soul and my broken heart. When I reached the state line, I stepped from my vehicle and spoke to the storm, "Peace Be Still!"

I drove towards my future with a promised forecast of never braving a storm alone, with strength for the journey and the umbrella of Faith to cover me in times of turmoil. From there forward, I did not look back at the storm in my rearview mirror but focused on the clear blue skies before me.

I am alive to give my testimony because I chose to Leave and Live. ~ KRBWM

P.S. – Please Leave and Live.

I was crying shortly after I started reading her testimony. I was weeping by the middle of it. I started moaning as I came to the end. I laid in my bed and knew that she had understood. She did know what I was going through because she had been through it too. I continued to cry until I had no tears. Then I just lay rocking in the fetal position until I lost track of time. I had to leave to live. I had to leave. I had to live.

I did not see the lady again during that hospital stay. I asked the nurses for her but they did not know who I was talking about. I asked all of the doctors about her too; but they did not know her either. I asked the cleaning staff and even the workers that bought my meals. No one knew who I was talking about. How in the world could that be?

This lady had just disappeared into thin air. I know that she had been here. She had touched me twice while in my room. I had seen her with my eyes, I know that I did. Besides that I was holding on to her pamphlet still. I read it over and over. I read it like it was medicine. Just maybe I might find my healing in there. I'd figured if he was sick, I had to be sick too. I'd let him get away with all of this. I needed my healing too.

It was weird but it seemed like the Lady did not want to be known. I should have asked her name. I mean who doesn't introduce themselves with a name? Well she didn't. She just gave me this pamphlet that I was holding on to like it was a baby's security blanket.

I really wished that I had talked to her now. But I had wasted the chance cause apparently she had come and gone. I should have told her that I felt trapped between wanting somebody to love me and staying in this mess that I had helped create. I know that I can do better, I just had to get to the point of no return before this whole thing veered off of the road and hit another oak tree. One oak tree was enough for me.

Usually people wanted something when they gave something. But I figured out pretty quickly that she just wanted to help me. She had wanted to share her story with the hopes that people in abusive relationships would leave and live. If that came about then her mission would be accomplished. I hoped that I would see her in the future and get a chance to tell her that I had read her story. I hoped that I would be able to tell her that I did leave.

Chapter 25

Crazy Gone?

That oak tree should have been enough but I guess it wasn't after all. Cause after a long hospital stay and a even longer recovery at my Mama's house; I was ready to go home. Home to my own house and to my man. Yes! I was going back. That demon had put all of the crazy away since hitting that oak tree. Hopefully it knocked it right out of him. I sure had not seen any of the crazy since I woke up in the hospital. Hopefully crazy was gone!

It was true that he had not come to visit the hospital the whole time that I was in there. He sent flowers, gifts, my favorite food and plenty of snacks. It looked like a funeral home it was so much flowers in my room. He kept them coming too. I had to give flowers away to other patients cause it was just too much. The food was too much. I didn't have a chance to get hungry. Before I could see what he sent more was coming. He had every member of his family and all of our friends cooking for me. It was a lot. But I was glad though that I could send plenty of those snacks to the churn when Mama came to visit. I wanted them to know that I was thinking of them constantly.

Everybody knew that hospital food was the worst. My aunts, family members and neighbors all worked in the hospital. Most of them worked in the kitchen too. Every single one of those women could burn those pots. They were some of the best cooks in the world. I had learned how to be the cook that I am from a lot of them. It wasn't anything that they could not make taste good.

But those hospital folks would not let those ladies cook for real. They had these bland, nasty and tasteless recipes that they had to follow to the letter. If they changed anything they could be fired and they needed those jobs too bad to disobey their bosses.

Salt and pepper could not revive that dead food. Maggots probably wouldn't have eaten it and they are known to eat anything. It was no wonder why people died up in here. They probably starved to death cause most of the food was no better than slop. Guess, no I know; that he wanted to keep me fat up.

All of the gifts, food and flowers was nice but it was also a reminder that he was out there waiting. I told myself that the old oak tree had changed us both. At least it seemed like it. It seemed like he was so grateful that I had lied to the doctors; not to mention the dreaded police. I know that he was so glad that he was walking the streets instead of being locked behind bars for years untold.

He pulled everything out of his best trick bag. That man showered me with every good thing that he could possibly think of. Lord knows that he had been sweet as sugar during my whole entire recovery. He'd brought me the prettiest flowers, the coldest drinks, the sweetest candy, the most desired snacks and scrumptious whole meals.

That man had sat on the couch holding my hand in the living room all evening long; just like we were love struck teenagers. He was more devoted than when we were courting. He never was far away in case I needed anything. If I mentioned anything then he made sure to get it for me. He was super nice to every single member of the family. He went above and beyond for my girls too. I thought that things had really truly changed and for the better too; since the day that oak tree got in our way.

So I ran right on back. Back to my fantasyland and sweet day dreams. It quickly turned into the worst nightmare I ever had. It took about a week until I found myself walking on eggshells. I was trying so hard to make things perfect. But I guess the ultimate lesson to learn is that nothing in this old tired world is perfect. As hard as we try, nothing and nobody is just right.

Trust and believe that those fragile precious eggshells broke soon enough. Probably cause they'd been cracked right from the start. I just did not want to see that they were damaged. Even what I did not see, I should have smelled. Those eggs and everything connected to them were rotten through and through.

After we were home together a few days; the real him strolled right out and reminded me exactly who he was. Absolutely nothing had changed. I had fallen for the devil's lies again. How could I have forgotten the truth? The devil was a liar. Always was. Totally is. Always will be.

That awful demon had me now and he knew it. It would be embarrassing to leave again and go back to my Mama when I had just gotten home to my house. Everybody warned me but I would not listen. I had told everyone how he had changed. I had defended him and lied for him. I had fooled myself into thinking that it was finally going to be different this time. I thought that I was getting my long awaited happily ever after. Instead; play-play was over. Here I was sitting in perjury with a evil devil and a life sentence.

A few days after we were home, I decided to make all of his favorites for breakfast. But he not having was not having to pretend or act nice anymore. He was at his very worst right away. Like he had tons to make up for his time of being nice. He screamed his head off that his coffee was not hot enough even though it had scolded my tongue when I tasted mine. He jumped up, sloshed the coffee all over the breakfast that I had worked so hard on, cause it had to be just right, you know?

I had made the bacon pretty as a magazine picture. The grits was creamy and had a pat of butter melting on top. The eggs were scrambled with a sprinkle of cheese on them just the way he loved them. I had big flaky homemade buttermilk biscuits just like Mama made. They were stacked on a platter with my homemade apple jelly and strawberry jam nearby. Had two big slices of honeyed ham that were browned so gently that they were making my mouth water. I even made sausage links that were saved from the last butchering. Fresh apples, oranges, cantaloupe, kiwis, strawberries, raspberries, blueberries and blackberries was all arranged nicely on a platter. There was enough food to feed an army even though it was just the two of us.

That breakfast would have rivaled one sold in the finest of restaurants, even if I say so myself. And with one flick of his temper, he totally ruined it. Guess it did not matter that it had taken me several hours while he slept to prepare and cook it for him.

I was checking that coffee's temperature and opened my mouth to say that I would heat his up if it needed it. I know that it did not need to be reheated. But I would have gladly done it to keep the peace. Before I could say one word, I saw the world shake like an earthquake was happening. I felt the table push into my gut and knock the wind right out of me. I could not believe that he was doing this again. We had agreed that crazy was gone forever but here it was making itself right at home again.

He knocked his chair down and moved so fast that I didn't even have time to react. I did not realize what was going to happen. I must have forgotten how quickly he could go from walking to clobbering me. I did not have time to run. There was no time to even cover my head or to protect myself in any way. I was trapped against the wall with a table in my stomach so tight that I could not breath.

I had believed him when he said that crazy had died at the foot of that old oak tree. I wanted it to be true so bad. Now I just wanted to run. I wanted everything to stop especially all of the pain. I was not ready for this. I wasn't.

I didn't even have time to pray. God knows everything. He is everywhere. I sure hoped that He would save me this day. In that split second I whimpered and uttered the surest prayer, "Jesus". Did not need any other words. With that one word, I said it all. I just hoped God heard me.

That demon ran towards me quickly, but I saw it all in slow motion. The gourmet breakfast smells were wafting up my nose. Between those smells and the table pushing my coffee up into my throat; I was sure that I was going to choke on my vomit. I closed my eyes for a mere moment. But I opened them quickly because I know that I needed to see what was going on.

He raised his hand as he came towards me and I saw exactly what was coming. Opening and closing. Flexing and stretching. I wasn't sure if it was going to be fists or fingers but it was happening, that is for sure. That demon slapped me so hard on that beautiful sunny morning that my head hit the wall and all I could see was stars like it was the darkest of nights.

That was bad but the look on my face must have ignited him more. I was looking right at him and it was not fear that he was seeing. He was seeing that I was not afraid. I made up my mind then and there; when I got from behind this table he was going to get some of what he was always giving.

He hit me with his fist up side my head so many times that I stopped counting. When I came too, cause I must have fainted sometime during the beating; all I could do was groan. I was still trapped by the kitchen table but I was a bloody mess.

When I could think again I reached up and grabbed my forehead. My head was hurting like someone had hit me with a hammer. Maybe five or six hammers if my head had any say so. Lordy, Lordy! I had the biggest fattest goose egg right on my noggin in the whole wide world.

When I was done vomiting on my beautiful breakfast remains and I could finally focus; I just started shaking. I looked around and saw that he was on his knees in front of me, begging and pleading. His words were coming so fast that I couldn't even make them out. I wasn't sure if it was how fast he was talking or how bad my head was hurting. I was sure that I had a bad concussion because I could see two devils instead of one. The last thing that I needed was two of this devil. The last thing that I needed was any devil.

By the time my three little girls came home from a sleep over with the neighbor girls, I had a beautiful scarf tied like an African head wrap around my hair. It was pulled low over my forehead with the bows all tied over the lump so that it stayed hidden. Didn't want to scare my babies with this baseball on my head. I know that it scared the hell out of me when I looked at it in the mirror. I was glad that my oldest lived with my Mama, cause she would not have been fooled by this scarf. My other girls probably wasn't either.

This was the end for me. I was finally sure of it. I was done. I had to go. Today was the end. I guess just like the Lady from the hospital, I was ready for my own share of "Peace Be Still".

Chapter 26

Jump Overboard

That lump on my head had me foggy for a time but my heart was feeling clear for the first time in forever. I needed to get over this and leave right on out of here. I was over him. Way, way over him. This ship had sailed off into the night early that morning at the breakfast table. It was time for me to walk the plank alone. I finally had to admit it to myself. This was never going to get any better. Never ever going to get any better. This big lump hiding under my bright pleated scarf was all of the proof that I would ever need of that.

I was finally ready to jump overboard with no life jacket. The water was ice cold and very dangerous out in the big bad world. I know it was not going to be easy jumping into the deep cause I ain't never swam a day in my life; especially by myself. But I was finally ready to learn. Hell I was ready to do it. Even if I was able to swim or not.

Now I know that it took me a while. But I was really serious this time. I'd said I was leaving this horrible mess for years. I'd promised family, friends, my girls and myself only to turn around and go right back to the same old thing.   All I know is that this was it.   I was done.   I was really, completely and finally done.

I'd ultimately reached the point of no return.   I was completely, thoroughly, unadulteratedly finished.   This was it.   The beginning of my forever.   I thought "I am done" to myself over and over.   It became a mantra as I repeated it in my head.   It was strengthening me to get out of this profuse torment.   I grabbed a real old suitcase. I threw a few outfits, some unders, some personals and slammed the bag shut.   When that old lock clicked shut, it locked that demon out of my heart for good and for real.

Every person that knew me knew how stubborn I could be.   I would stick to my point like cement.   Once I made up my mind about a thing, it took all of heaven and God Himself to get me to change my mind. And my mind was all made up.   That lump was the straw.   I wasn't waiting around no more for it to break my back. That lump was going to be the last lump that I was ever going to take from him. That lump was my ticket out of this hell. I just needed to get him out of my house, out of my heart, out of my life; but most importantly, out of my head.

I packed some stuff in a bag for my girls. Thought we'd go over to Mama's house cause she'd gone to visit one of my sisters out of town for two weeks. That would give him a minute to find some where to go. Didn't know where or what he was going to do. For once, I can honestly say that I just didn't care. He had to go. That's all to it, he had to go. And I really meant it.

I was not scared of him. So when he walked in I had those bags by the door. I told him that I was going to Mama's for a while and that by the time that I came back he needed to be gone. The tears, begging and pleading didn't do nothing this time. His ticket was revoked for entry to my heart. Yep, it was done.
Ain't nothing was working for him. It was never going to work again. I was cold as ice and serious as all get out. Time to put the devil out for good. Yes! He had to go. He could go anywhere, even back to hell where he came from. I just did not care as long as he got away from me. Cause he was not going to live here anymore. Game over.

I shook him off like a rag doll when he tried to pull me back by my arm. I looked out at my girls peeking from the back seat of my friend's car and pushed him down on the floor. I put my finger in his face and saw the fear roll up in his eyes. Why had I let this cowardly scared weasel do all those painful things to me for all of those years?

I told him that he had seven days to be out of my house and my life. I let him know if I saw him before then I would beat the bricks off of him; no matter where we were. I told him that it was over. As he whimpered on the floor like the bug that he was, I could see that he knew it was true this time. I could squash him and for once he knew it. Ain't no love lived here anymore.

I stayed at Mama's house for several days. I had peace and everything was alright. I started thinking of a future without him and I was alright with that. I was seeing what I could be without him and it was good.

It didn't take long before I ran into a couple of problems though. When I was packing so quickly, I realized that I didn't pack good enough. I had not planned either. I had no money and needed some essentials. Everything that I needed was at home but the devil was probably still at my house.

It was only day six and he was going to have to be thrown out cause he was not going to leave on his own. I planned to get my uncles together who had wanted to throw him out on his butt for many years. Well now they could do just that.

I know that Mama did not spend a lot of money on food when she was going to visit one of my sisters cause she wanted a little extra in her hands in case she and the kids wanted to do something special. I had packed clothes but didn't get enough food and other supplies.

A few more days went by at Mama's house and the food ran real low. I was going to have to go back to my house and get some. Didn't have no extra money to go to the store. And I was not going to run up the credit bill when I already had the stuff I needed at my house. Hell it was my house. I was going to go and get my food and other things that I needed.

So I asked one of Mama's neighbors for a ride back to my house to grab some food. My three girls piled into the back and waited while I pulled the house door closed. I was not going to fight him in front of my girls. I would get what I needed, leave and wait until Mama was back. Then I would put that devil out for good.

My three girls sat in the back seat of my friend's car acting like little girls do. I had three back there but I've got four. Never could leave my oldest daughter out. She was with Mama on their little vacation. Even though she'd always lived with Mama; that girl came to visit me all the time. I was happy that we were close. We were friends. We did good with that one. Especially since she was a teenager in high school and now dating. She came by regularly with her boyfriend. They didn't always have money but they could come by and eat good and listen to music at my place.

I even offered them a beer on occasion. The legal drinking age is 18 and she was almost there. He was over 18 and was always happy to be treated like an adult. I would just rather them drink over here and be safe than get in trouble out there.

People might think that's crazy but I wanted them safe rather than sneaking around out there and finding themselves in dangerous situations. Didn't want them drinking and driving or nothing crazy. Besides that the devil did not act crazy around my oldest. It was like she had something that kept him in check. He might have growled now and then but he did not roar and definitely did not bite around her.

The good thing was that my oldest girl was not a drinker or a rule breaker. She was a good girl. She would be alright. That holy oil that Mama had poured on her when she was born was strong stuff. It was still working good cause she was a church girl all the way through. My Mama had gotten Jesus deep in there. Man, she was as serious about God as Mama was. That was a good thing too.

Me and Mama had done alright raising her. She would do good things in this world. At least I hoped so. I hoped that looking at me living this crazy life while she was growing up had not messed her or the other girls up too bad. I hoped that they learned from my life. More than anything I prayed that they would never ever repeat it. I was believing that just maybe they would learn the most out of me leaving this craziness.

Chapter 27

Crazy Is Back!

My friend drove slow as molasses. When we finally pulled into my yard it looked like the party of the year was going on. What the hell? This man had lost his crazy mind! There were men everywhere. The barbecue was going in the yard. Guys had full plates and cold drinks. They were laughing and joking like this was the best day ever. They were eating all my food and absolutely tearing up my house.

Jesus! Crazy was back! My beautiful, totally "just right" house was a wreck. It was destroyed. Every place I looked, all I could see was the trash, plates, waste, cups and spills. I could not believe my eyes. He knew that my house was a big deal. At least it was a big deal to me.

I never let anything be out of place. But here my lovely house was; all tore up from the floor up. I could hardly breathe. The loud booming base filled music that they were jamming like it was a disco or a juke joint or something was almost more than I could bare. I could not take this. I was about to freak the hell out. As I walked through, I just knew that I was going to lose my mind.

Those men out in the yard ran like the devil himself was behind them when they saw me. They got out of dodge fast, quick and in a hurry. They were having a ball until they realized that I could see each and every one of them. They knew that I could break their necks if I got close to any of them. They were scaredy-cats deep down and now they were running for cover.

Then that devil walked around the corner of the yard and approached me. That devil had the nerves to ask why I was even here. Why I was here? Ain't that a trip? Why I was at my own house? What? Before I could even reply, he started cursing and calling me every low name under the sun. He might have called me some that I did not even know. I could not believe him. This had to be a joke.

I started laughing, even though tears were coming down my cheeks. Whenever I was furious, those tears would start flowing. I did not even realize that I was crying. I guess I couldn't help but cry because every where around me the house was destroyed.

Then that devil went fool. That little shrimp tried to act like a big man. He shoved me towards the car that I had just come in. He was trying to show off in front of the men that were still watching as they ran off. But today was not his day. That last lump on my head was the period on his pain list for me. I could not even think of letting him get away with putting his hands on me again.

I was all the way finished. I was done. Done with all this. Done with him. I shoved him back with all of my "Done". He flew onto the ground and slid across the grass on his flat little behind. I started to go over there and beat the tar out of him. I started to see how much pain he could bare. He was good at dishing it out so I wondered if he could take any.

But no! I decided I was not doing that in front of my little girls that were peeking out of the windows of my friend's car. I looked down at him on the ground with my meanest stare daring him to get up. That look told him that I wanted him to get up so that I could give him a little payback. He stayed down there staring like he couldn't believe what had just happened while all of his drunk friends stopped running long enough to laugh at

227

him. When I stood with my hands on my hips and glanced around, every one of them that my eyes landed on, started running again.

Then I brushed my hands off and stepped over that garbage on the ground. I looked back down at him to make sure that he had not moved. Guess I was looking for any excuse to beat him to a pulp and kick the little bit of butt that he had. But he was still laying on the ground with only his mouth moving. He looked like a fish trying to wait for food. No words or no noises came out. He was probably in shock. But I am beyond sure that he got the message this time: "I'm leaving."

I shook my head and went into my house. I started throwing drunk guys out from the front door and at every step. It did not take much because they got scared sober when they saw me and scuttled towards any exit. A few even went out of the windows. I emptied the house of the vermin real fast. I went to every room and made sure to put every last one out.

Then I decided that he would be leaving today too. His time was up. I grabbed a bag threw a few of his things into it and slung it out of the front door as hard and as fast as I could. Those guys that were falling out of windows and doors started laughing their heads off. That old suitcase landed on the grass and busted open. His drawers and closed flew out all over the grass. He was no longer on the grass so maybe he had slithered off to hide.

I locked the front door and closed all of the windows. I was not in the mood for more drama today and I could not stay in my house with it looking like this. This mess would make me crack up. I would just get the food, the supplies and head back to Mama's. I could clean up my house later.

In the midst of all of this mess, I was feeling empowered. How could that be when everything are me was in chaos? I guess the good feelings came from taking my life back from the devil. I just wanted to have a good life. I just wanted to be happy. I just wanted to be loved. I just wanted to leave. I just wanted to live. I deserved to love, leave and live.

I made it to the kitchen and grabbed a couple of plastic bags. I started throwing can goods in. My sink was filled with dirty dishes. Pots, pans, bowls and food littered every surface including the floor. This idiot really was mental. He knew how I felt about my house and yet he had it trashed. Made me want to go out there and trash him.

I was so very sad. I was terribly hurt. More than anything though, I was mad as hell. Whenever I was mad, I blubbered like a baby. Here I was packing food like I was a bagger at the grocery store and snotting my brains out. I couldn't help it no matter how hard I tried.

The tears were flowing so hard and fast that I could hardly even see what I was doing. I was not giving him one more day. No! Not one more! Enough was enough! I just wanted peace. He better be gone. Gone right now. Gone from my house. Gone from my life. Just gone.

Chapter 28

The Bullet's Name

I heard my three girls yelling and screaming. Now, I know he was not messing with my girls. All of the hell that I was holding in was about to rain down on him. As I turned, I heard the large bay kitchen window squeak open.

Why were the girls screaming like that? I know that he was not bothering my babies. That was the last thing that he wanted to do. If he bothered one hair on their heads, I was going to jail for murder. I promise that. Gonna kill him dead.

This day was finally here. The day that I was completely done. The day that I was really leaving. I was going to be done today for me and for my girls. I should've been left. Why had I wasted all these years on this little bit of a man? Mama always said that the devil comes to kill, steal and destroy. Well he had done all of that in my life and I was declaring that it was enough. Nope he was not doing another thing.

I was done dealing with him! No more. He was getting put out today. I turned from the cabinet as I heard the loud ear splitting boom. I saw the bullet. I saw it. It was coming in slow motion. That bullet was coming directly at me. There was no place to run or hide. It was coming for me. The devil was taking his final shot cause if I lived...

He had pulled the trigger on that old sawed-off shotgun that I refused to let him bring in my house. He really did it. Have Mercy, Lord! They said that bullets done have names. But that is a lie; cause this bullet had my name on it.

I wonder what made this time different than all of the other times? How many times had I been hit in the head with that shotgun? I had been pistol whipped with the Colt 45 that he kept in the car's glovebox several times.

I had lost several teeth when he hit me in the mouth with the barrel of the 45. When I spit those teeth out along with all of the blood onto his white shirt then he had started crying and begging. I never smiled the same after that. Always smiled with my mouth shut cause I did not want people to see those missing teeth.

One Saturday night he had been drinking all day long. I figured it was not going to be a good night so when one of my brothers and his girlfriend stopped by, I sent my girls over to Mama to spend the night. Good thing too. He was on a special kind of crazy that night.

He told me that a bullet was in the cylinder of the 45 and he would twirl that cylinder and click it close. Then he would tell me how bad my dinner had been; which was a bald-faced lie; then he would point the gun at me and pull the trigger. The click would sound like lightning striking the earth.

God had protected me that night cause I lost count of how many times, he pulled that trigger. But the bullet, God help me; was never in the right place to hurt me. I could have lost my life and my mind that night. But the begging was pitiful and he had thrown the gun in the marsh out back.

I realized now long afterwards that the gun had not stayed in the marsh. One evening after a bunch of our friends and family had gone home from a thrown together barbeque, the evil came back with a vengeance.

I had shed tears and sweat like a pig when he stuffed one of those guns in my mouth and held the other to my head as he threatened to kill me on that occasion. But he had never done it. Why now? Why now had he pulled the trigger with a bullet in the chamber?

Those guns made him feel like a big bad man. He had little man issues and carrying around guns made him feel powerful or something. I hated him having them around and never allowed them in the house. But he kept them in his car at all times. I wish that I had made sure that he had gotten rid of them after the last time that he threatened me.

After the normal flood of tears and pitiful begging that he did after his episodes; he had promised to give both of the guns away. I never asked if he had done it. I should have. I should have given them away myself. Now those guns along with that speeding bullet that was coming at me were going to be the death of me.

Oh Lord God, NO! I can't believe this. That bullet had my name on it. I had stayed too long. This was all hitting home but that bullet was bringing the realization way too late. I was going to lose everything when that bullet landed. This was my ending and it was coming way too soon.

Sadly it was all ending in my pretty kitchen that I had cooked thousands of meals in to fill the stomachs and hearts of the people that I love. All of my hopes and dreams was being stopped right here at my shiny white farmhouse sink by a tiny piece of metal and a dash of gun powder.

Here I was being taken out by this devil cause I had played pity-pat with him for too long. I knew better but I had not done better. So it was time to face the consequences of all of my choices. My forever started today. It was not the forever that I thought that I was going to have, that is for sure.

Oh Lord, I was not going to see my Mama again on this earth. I was going to have to wait for her in Heaven. What are we going to do without each other? Jesus, God!

I was not going to be here to help raise my girls. The oldest was almost grown but my other three were still little girls. I would not be with any of them for the special moments. No more birthdays, no more graduations, no weddings, no celebrations.

I would never even know my grandchildren. I did not know what my girls would grow up to be. I was not going to see them as Women. I would never see the places they would go. I would not know the changes that they would make in this world.

What had I done, God? All of my decisions had led to this moment. Forever was on the way to me. Forever was almost here. All I could think was I could have made other choices. I should have made better choices. I should have made any other choice.

I could have gone right instead of left. I could have lived and not died. I could have left long before that bullet entered or left the chamber. I always knew things could end this way. I just never believed it would happen to me. That stupid, fake, stinky thinking was killing me. Oh God! It was killing me now; right now - today.

Daddy God, I was not going to be here for the hard times; the scary time or the good times. I was not going to be able to protect my little girls. I would not be able to encourage them.

I was not going to be able to help them either. I was not going to be able to comfort them. I would never be able to celebrate with them. I was losing it all. I was losing everything. I was dying today because I chose to stay too long.

This man was taking every good thing away from me. This devil was taking my babies' Mama away. He was taking away my parents' oldest child. I was going away from my Mama, my girls, my sisters and brothers, my family and my friends. Forever was going to start right now.

I already knew that I was leaving the earth when that bullet landed. That bullet was my ride to Glory. That bullet was going to be my ticket into the pearly gates. I was going to meet God up close and personal real soon. I wasn't even considering the pain or the hurting that I could face. None of that mattered right now.

I could only think about the pain, trauma and hurting that my family and friends was going to go through cause

I had stayed too long. If only I had left. If only I had left safely.

Well with my last breath I prayed to God for forgiveness. I prayed that he would take care of my girls, my Mama and my family. I prayed that others in situations like mine would leave and live so that they could have real love.

I would bare the years of abuse, pain and trauma all over again to stay here with the people I loved or at least to save them from the pain that the bullet was bringing to all of us. But God was done making bargains with me. He was giving me my last few seconds to realize my greatest mistakes.

I knew that God was right here with me cause He was a forgiving, Why hadn't I left long ago when he was emotionally abusive? I could have been gone so many times before; especially when he opened the physical and sexual abuse doors. Why had I stayed through any abuse? Why had I put up with all of the atrocities that he had reeked on me, my girls and my family? Why Lord, oh why?

I could see the brightest blinding beautiful lights getting ever closer as that bullet approached. I was not afraid cause I knew without a doubt that God is always with me. I was in the valley of the shadow of death and God's Angels were all around me. I was not alone.

I have always known that God is Love and Love is God. God is omnipotent and omnipresent. He is all around us. He is in us. So when I am in God, everybody that I love, I will live in them. As long as they call my name, think of me, remember me and tell my story; then I will not be forgotten. I will never forget them. I will carry them with me for all of eternity. That's for sure. I was going to be alright because today when I left this body; I would be with God for all time.

I just wanted more time. I needed more time. More time to love. More time to leave. More time to live. I wished that I could tell my Mama how sorry I am that I did not listen better when she warned me about this devil. I wish that I could talk to her especially to let her know how much I love her, one more time.

I wish that I could kiss my girls, sing them to sleep, braid their hair, sew them pretty dresses and cook their favorite foods. I wish that I could fix my sisters' hair in the styles from magazines and help them fix up a outfit to look chic and cool before they went out with their friends.

I wish that I could play baseball, kickball, dodgeball and basketball in the yard with my little brothers. I wish that I had time to make freezy-pops for all of the neighborhood kids and watch them play in the water to cool off as they enjoyed themselves in the heat of the day. I wish that I had time to sit with my Daddy and listen to his stories of times gone by. I wish... I wish... I wish.

I spent a split second praying better for those that looked at my life after I was gone. Today I would be gone. I could have done this different. I could have left safely. I could have lived. I prayed that others do not make the same mistakes that I made. I was hoping that they got out of their situation before it was too late.

I was praying that the people that heard my story, see a good woman that loved and wanted to be loved. I was praying that they would learn from my choices; good, bad and ugly.

I prayed that because of my mistakes; prayerfully they would choose life. I was praying that if one person listened, learned and decided to "Safely" leave abuse; than my life nor my death would be in vain.

In that last instance, I whispered, "Father God take care of my babies, my Mama and my family til we meet again in the great by and by. Let them know that I will love them for eternity and beyond. Please Daddy God, receive all of me into Your hands." The bullet was coming faster and faster now.

The three little girls were running as fast as their legs could carry them. I heard their voices yelling. I knew that I could not keep them safe once that bullet touched down.

One more prayer, "Lord keep my family safe! Please God!" It was already too late, they just didn't know it. They were running, breathing loudly and screaming at the top of their lungs: "Mama! Mama! He's got a gun! Run Mama! A gun Mama! He has a real gun Mama! Mama! Mama! Mama!"

The last thing that I heard on the earth was three of my four girls screaming my highest badge of honor – "Mama". As I turned, a loud boom cracked and the bullet arrived as I called out to Jesus. The bullet hit me in the forehead and knocked me to the floor. Sorrowful tears still streamed down my face as I closed my eyes for the last time and still more continued to mix with the blood that flowed from the bullet hole, long after I took my last breath.

Epilogue

<u>Say Her Name!</u>

Three young girls at a small country church cemetery are kneeling at a grave as they place handpicked flowers on the simple cement headstone. A lady dressed in white is humming as she looks on from far away in the shadows across the yard. She is such a glorious vision with the sun shining on her that she appears to be glowing. She quietly sings a song that echos as it rides along on the sweet summer breeze.

The oldest daughter walks across the grass towards the gravestone wearing a Graduation cap and gown. She takes the graduation cap off, kisses it and places it on the headstone. It wobbles but jauntily hangs on the corner of the tombstone. The cap has a music symbols painted around the words, "WE All did it!"

She unzips the graduation gown and folds it neatly. She places it on the grave's vault. Underneath the graduation gown, she has on US Army Fatigues and Army boots. She reaches into the cargo pocket of her pants, takes out a hat and puts it on. She turns to the headstone, blows kisses to the sky and salutes.

She hugs her Granny hard and thanks her for everything that she has ever done and all that she will do. She holds hands with her Granny as they watch the three girls making crowns out of the tiny flowers that surround the grave.

She looks at her Granny for assurance. Granny smiles a makes a promise with her oldest granddaughter; realizing that she had made once the same promise with her oldest daughter. The reassurance that the two of them can raise these girls real good. They both smile and agree.

They call out to the girls that it is time to go now. As the little ones skip and run all around her; she holds her hands out to her little sisters. They all stand, clasps hands and all blow a few sweet farewell kisses to the bright blue sunny sky.

The oldest daughter looks down at the grave and says, "We will take care of each other. We will tell the world your name. We will tell them your story. We will tell them to love, leave and live." She stands straighter, pushes her shoulders back, turns her eyes to the sky one more time.

Granny whispers, "Say her name." In unison, all of the girls stand and call out her name to the sky several times. Granny and the oldest watch smiling as the little girls blow kisses over and over as they twirl and laugh.

As they turn to leave, the singing Lady in white; throws pale pink, passionate purple, fiery orange, dark streaked red and creamy white flowers on them like tiny kisses. The girls look around in awe as they wonder where the flowers are coming from.

They are surrounded in the sweetest scents. The oldest looks to Granny who has tears running down her face. They both recognize the scent of her Mother's favorite perfume. Then the oldest smiles as the three girls twirl and dance in the shower of colors as the wind continuously blows the flowers all around them. Granny whispers, "She is here with us and will be with us always."

Each girl including the oldest, reaches for their favorite colors. As the petals settle all around the grave, they each promise to be more than she dreamed they could be. They promise to make her proud. They promise to be the women that she expected them to be. They promise to be all that God intended when they were birthed into the earth.

The clouds pass in front of the sun for a few moments as if it is a reminder that darkness comes but together they can make it through anything. Then just as quickly the sun comes out brightly again to reinforce the promise that joy will come again.

The Lady remains in the shadows that turn darker until the white of her dress blowing in the wind is barely seen. The sun shines it's brightest on and in front of the girls. The girls tightly hold hands in a show of love, unity, bravery, pride and hope.

The little ones skip and giggle as they go off into the bright light of their futures without their Mother here but with each of them holding pieces of her within themselves that they will forever treasure and amplify into their lives.

Each of them will ensure that her life nor her death is in vane. Her girls will forever have her in their minds, on their lips and in their hearts.

This is not the end...

This is just the Promise of our Beginning!

In Loving Memory
Of Trr!

Patricia Ann Geddis

Each of them will ensure that her life nor her death is in Vane. Her girls will forever have her in their minds, on their lips and in their hearts.

This is not the end....

This is just the Promise of our Beginning!

Author's Notes

Melody Geddis McFadden is the oldest daughter of Patricia Ann Geddis. She gave me life and my name. I am grateful for the opportunity to tell the world her name. I am a loving Wife, Mother and MeMe that loves my family with all of me.

I live a life of service. I am – a US Army Veteran, a Everytown for Gun Safety, Surrogate National Speaker, a Sr. Survivor Fellow, a member of the Everytown's National Veterans Advisory Council the Moms Demand Action's SC Faith Outreach Lead, an avid supporter and Volunteer for Newtown Action Alliances, a supporter of Brady's, Giffords as well as other gun violence prevention groups and a passionate advocate for Peace and a better world.

In my personal capacity I am an Ordained Minister, Counselor and Founder of Blessed Ministries, Blessed Devotions and Survivor Smiles. I have chosen the blessings, by harnessing power from severe pain and purposing to honor my loved ones (Patricia Ann Geddis, Sandy Pa'Trice Geddis Barnwell, L'Oreal Bowman, Corey Gee Glenn) and all others that have been taken in senseless gun violence with a life of devoted service; thereby ensuring that their lives nor their deaths are in vain. If I were to name all of those taken in senseless gun violence since the gun violence epidemic began, there would not be enough pages or ink.

The contents of this writing is based on actual events, memories, conversations, observations and situations that occurred in my life and in my Mother's life. These events although based on real events are placed in fictional content as my Mother truly died from Gun Violence while living in a Domestic Violence Tragedy. Although she did not get to see her girls grow up; they are all successful, healthy, loving women. They are each making a difference in the world. They are reminding the world that she was indeed – Here.

Every single person that we help is proof of my Mother's generosity, kindness, life views and loving heart. If she saw a need, she met it. She placed others before herself and would never hesitate to help if needed. I often remind people that we did not lose her. We did not let her go willingly. We were victimized children. Out Mother was "Taken" from us.

Because she was taken by an illegal sawed off shotgun; I am a Survivor, a Gun Violence Prevention Advocate and a

Founder of Blessed Ministries where I serve as a Pastor and Minister that has always prioritized healing for Women, Children and Families that live in Abusive situations. Each one that is taken in abuse we Honor with Action. Each one that I help change their lives is a tribute to my Mother's memory. Each one that leaves abuse and chooses life is a Blessing.

I would like to Thank my Family for their love, support, compassion and empathetic understanding. These memories are truly my own. Understand that they are the memories of a traumatized child that witnessed abuse far too many times. These conversations and observations may have been private or witnessed by some of them as well. But this is my own truth. I do understand that traumatized children sometimes view situations through skewed and even foggy lenses. I also realize that some family members may remember certain details of events portrayed here differently. It is alright to do so. This is my own version of those shared events. These memories are my own.

Family, please understand that in writing about these memories, I do not intend to blame, embarrass, shame or infer guilt. I have not told your versions or asked for your stories. This was my story to tell. It is with a sincere purpose to save lives. I also seek my own healing for the little girl that lives in me that experienced and witnessed the abuse that my Mother lived and died in. I pray that others are healed. My desire is never to Hurt; only and always to Honor. My love is pure and true. My heart and mind is clear. Family, I love you then, now and for all time.

I have tried to prevent the further victimization of family members and friends by using anonymous characters. I would prefer that those living in Domestic Violence; see themselves. Then prayerfully they can see themselves leaving before their own lives are taken. In that anonymity is the opportunity for confrontation, truth, decisions and healing. I plead with readers if abuse is your situation, then please choose life.

I have incorporated my faith, education, life experiences, advocacy, volunteer labor and trauma work with abuse victims, Victors, Survivors and Overcomers to ensure that this accounting of these abusive situations do not damage but absolutely liberate. My prayer is that through this peek into our lives that they can see the way out of their own abuse to freedom.

The Pamphlet: (The Eye Of My Storms - My Test Became My Testimony) that was included during the hospital scene is based on actual events of a Domestic Violence Victor. Katherine Morris chose to leave and live. She bases her life of Faith and Ministry on the decision to never go back. It is her life goal of gratitude for her deliverance from Domestic Violence to Minister to Women, Children and Families that live in abusive situations that she experienced first-hand. She found that sharing some of the abuse that she overcame has been cathartic and healing for areas that she thought long ago healed. She is and I am extremely grateful that she opened these private places to us so that others might not stay in abuse but choose another path. She chose to share her story so that others will witness an Overcomer that they can emulate, who has realized the dream of finding real love and is now living in love, in healing, in health and in happiness.

This is my Mother's story. I'm grateful for the opportunity to let the world know some of her. Sadly people will see a lot of the times that were extremely painful. That pain is shared in hopes of saving others from the life that she lived and the death that she died. I do want to assure everyone that there were many wonderful, sweet, happy moments as well.

Those cherished memories have contributed to the Woman that I am. I want to make it very clear that I forgive my Mother for her choices, weaknesses, shortcomings and for every moment that I wished she was still here for. I thank her for her love, for every good that she did for me and for everything that she gave to me. I love her eternally.

Most importantly, I'd like to express my gratitude to God for the husband, children and grandchildren that He has shared with me. Ultimately, they belong to Him. I am humble that He has entrusted them to me to Mother and to love. They are my life and my legacy. I desire a better world for all of them. It is with my whole heart, mind, body and soul that I strive to be apart of making the world safer, better and more full of love for each of them. I pray that they never forget that I believe that God is Love... Love is a verb... Love is action... Love is for always.

This book is my prayer that Senseless Gun Violence will end and all of those Taken will be Remembered, Loved and Honored with Action! My prayer is also for all of those living in Domestic Violence that they might find Love, Leave and Live. My prayer is for strength, endurance, more than enough, double for the trouble and endless resilience for every Advocate fighting to make this world better. With Love, Smiles & Every Blessing! ~ Melody Geddis McFadden

<u>Reflections</u>

Reflections

Reflections

Reflections

Reflections

Advocacy

Please Visit & Support

Blessed Devotions
https://www.facebook.com/groups/BlessedMinistriesDevotions/

Survivor Smiles
https://www.facebook.com/groups/377194210037944/?ref=share

EveryTown
https://www.everytown.org/

Mom's Demand Action
https://momsdemandaction.org/

Bullets4Life
http://bullets4life.org/

Taking Back Our Village
https://m.facebook.com/tbourvillage365/

We Are Their Voices
https://www.wearetheirvoices.com/
https://www.facebook.com/WeAreTheirVoices/

Newtown Action Alliance
https://www.newtownactionalliance.org/

Brady
https://www.bradyunited.org/

Giffords
https://giffords.org/lawcenter/gun-laws/

Find a place to Serve!

Doing nothing – Changes nothing. - by Melody

Honor With ACTION!

End Gun Violence & Domestic Violence!

At 17, life forever changed and forced me to become an adult. I had to help take care of my three little sisters, who saw our mother shot and killed by her boyfriend.

—Melody Geddis McFadden

everytown.org/momentsthatsurvive

Call Crime Stoppers
ANONYMOUSLY!
843-554-1111

www.ingramcontent.com/pod-product-compliance
Lightning Source LLC
Chambersburg PA
CBHW070457030726

47503CB00004B/1082